HIDDEN HEARTS

STOLEN LEGACY, BOOK THREE

CANDICE BUNDY

PIPER FOX

CONTENTS

THE MOON IN THE MAZE

SERA

I strode through the faery portal, with Marcos following just a couple of steps behind me. Hedgerows flanked our path, looming at least ten or eleven feet high and dense enough that little light shone through. Despite the sun still high overhead, the walkway was in deep shadow.

I heard the portal whoosh shut behind us, but I didn't bother looking back. The task at hand lay ahead of me, and honestly if I'd stood there facing off with Taneisha one second longer... Well, I didn't want to think about what I might have done, even knowing I wasn't strong enough to beat the fae.

But instead of trying to zap her ass, I'd threatened the fae with war. I searched my heart, wondering what had come over me. My mind had been advising caution and strategy, but my heart said the fae had gone too far and I wanted Taneisha to pay. I wondered how my family would feel if the threat of war materialized. The Lowes were never ones to back down from a fight, but I didn't imagine they'd love me drawing them into a conflict where they had little to gain beyond defending the family honor.

Yeah. I sure as hell wanted war. But first, we had to win back the rest of the posse's legacies. Taneisha had pulled trick after trick on the other quests, and I was convinced this hedge maze would somehow be even worse.

Up ahead Franc had a wild-eyed Emrys by the scruff while Liam and Caden stood to either side, no doubt ready to catch the half-mad demi-god if he slipped from Franc's grasp. Watching Emrys twist and strain against Franc, a wholly inappropriate image filled my mind. I knew Franc and Caden played that way. Was it too much to wonder if Em and Franc did, too? I shook my head. I needed to keep my focus on the hunt, not wondering how much oil you'd need to lubricate a round of naked wrestling between two demi-gods.

Just as we reached the others, a deep-toned gong rang through the air, reverberating so powerfully I felt the vibration hit me like a gut-punch. I wobbled on my feet, and then stopped short of reaching the others, needing to wait until the sensation passed.

Speaking of tricks; what the hell was that about?

Marcos moved close, dropping our bags to the ground so he could slide his arms around me, steadying me on my feet. I leaned into his strength, resting my forehead on his chest as I gasped for breath.

"A gong?" I choked out, gasping my words as my chest ached. "As if that isn't corny as hell."

"Might be corny, but as we've learned on these quests, that doesn't mean we shouldn't take it seriously. You okay?" Marcos asked.

I shrugged. "I think so? It feels like something kicked

me in the gut." I looked up, finding five sets of eyes focused squarely on me, including Emrys. As they looked at me, a frisson ran down my spine as I shivered under their attention. Trying to shake off the intensity of the sensation, I took a deep breath and pushed away from Marcos, but he resisted, holding me tight in his arms.

"You sure you're steady on your feet again?" he asked, his voice low and raspy.

When I glanced up at Marcos, the raw emotion in his eyes gave me pause. "The pain is fading. You don't need to worry about me so much, Marcos. I'll be fine."

Marcos leaned in, running his nose along my neck as he breathed in deep. A chill ran over my skin as a heat flared between my thighs. He held still, and I had the impression he was holding something back.

"What is it?" I asked him.

He looked me in the eye and arched his brow. "For someone who doesn't want her mates to claim her, you sure didn't hesitate to draw a line in the sand with Taneisha to protect us."

Wait, what? My jaw dropped as my brain did somersaults.

"You were fantastic back there staring down Taneisha. Also, proprietary as all hell." Marcos chuckled, and then planted a kiss on my cheek before releasing me and taking a step back. "I'll give you a moment."

Which was lucky for me, because I was totally out of words. Sure, I thought of them as my guys. My posse. But fated mates? It was ludicrous. Impossible.

Right?

I got busy stuffing things from my old backpack into the new one, hoping the moment would pass. Something momentarily drew my attention to Franc, who stood in front of Emrys, fingers kneading his temples as they stared each other down. It was a tense, private moment, and I couldn't help but look away, wondering what demi-god dynamic I'd just glimpsed.

"What did Sera do?" Liam asked, concern creasing his brow as his eyes flashed with a lupine yellow. He rose to his feet, hooking his backpack over his shoulder. If Liam wasn't careful, he was going to earn some wrinkles just worrying over me.

At last, I found words. "Nothing. It was nothing."

Marcos set his hands on his hips, his expression filled with a mix of admiration and humor. "Our quirky little mage faced off with Taneisha. Told her she'd had enough and said if the fae allowed any of us to die, Sera would sic her entire mage family on her. Taneisha accepted, so we're all under Sera's, and by extension the Lowe's, protection now."

Caden, who'd been sorting through his bag, pulled out some fresh clothes. Brazen as ever, he stripped down to his boxers before pulling on his pants, his form fitting briefs leaving little to the imagination. "Aw, it sounds like we're finally growing on you," he said to me as he zipped up his new pleather pants. It did not surprise me that the demon would wear the bold choice, but I wondered why Taneisha made the choices she did when selecting gear and clothing for our bags.

Timing really was nine-tenths of humor, and by the bulge in the front of his pants, I had no illusions about what was growing on Caden. I couldn't help but laugh. Caden mocked being offended, holding a hand over his heart and pouting.

Liam tried to hide a satisfied smile and failed. He walked over to me, and when I rose with my bag in my hand, he was right in front of me. After the initial discovery of the marks on my shoulders, the marks he'd claimed were mating marks, Liam had made a point of giving me space. I'd suspected he hadn't wanted to push me too hard. There was also his absolute faith in fate, which he knew I didn't share.

There was an intense heat in his gaze when he spoke. It surprised me he didn't reach out and touch me or pull me into his embrace. "So, we're yours now?" he said, his voice an intimate whisper.

I rolled my eyes at the wolf shifter, but Liam's intensity didn't waver. "We're all in this together, wolf," I replied, refusing to answer his question. Refusing to whisper back. Why should I? The question was based on his conviction that we were all fated mates. I hadn't been able to convince him otherwise.

"Yes. We are. In more ways than one," he said, his voice a low rumble.

Despite my irritation with Liam for his insistence on doggedly coming back to this point of disagreement, I couldn't deny the growing attraction I had for him. For all of them, actually, but right now, Liam was the one up in my face. He hadn't been shaving, and his light scruff of a beard gave his face an even more rugged appeal. Truly, he was more attractive with it than without, and I bit my lower lip as I breathed in his musky scent.

I was going to miss them when the quests were over.

Yellow flashed in Liam's eyes, and I sensed his wolf hovered right underneath the surface. A shiver ran over my skin as I recalled stories of the unrelenting drive shifters felt to claim their fated mates. Was Liam fighting to hold back his beast every time we were close? Is that why he'd been giving me space?

Liam leaned in close and whispered into my ear, his breath hot on my neck. "You might not agree with me, but I notice you're not arguing either. Could it be that you're warming up to the idea?"

I knew he meant being his, well, their claimed mate, but all I could focus on was Liam's musky scent. Memories of Liam inside me when we were at the nature preserve flooded my mind, bringing a warm flush to my cheeks. Well, I was certainly warming to something.

I glanced around, seeing how everyone else's attention was focused on our conversation, even Franc and Emrys, who appeared done with whatever they'd been doing. All staring at us. At me. Waiting to hear what I'd say.

I took a step back, shaking my head to clear my thoughts. "There's nothing to argue about," I shot back. "Besides, we have more important things to worry about right now."

Liam's gaze turned stormy. "We can agree to disagree, at least for now." I half expected he'd continue to press the issue of my mating marks, but after a moment, he crossed his arms and sighed. "What would you like to know about my legacy?"

The unspoken tension in the group dissipated as the conversation turned toward Liam's legacy.

"Everything about it," I replied. "What does it look like? What does it mean to you? And any ideas why Taneisha might have chosen a maze for your quest?"

Liam's expression soured. "My legacy is a wolf's head carved from moonstone, the size of a silver dollar. It fits easily in the palm of my hand. I received it from my father after I'd run in my first hunt as an adolescent."

"So it's small enough it could be anywhere. Does the stone represent your coming of age within the pack?" I asked.

He nodded. "It's also magical, holding moonlight within it. I kept it close to me while we were at Goldenbriar. It helped me control my wolf despite being away from my pack and the wilds of the forest. I've kept it with me for years."

"Do you or your wolf depend upon it?" I asked. "I mean, what will happen if we can't get it back?"

"No, we don't. But it's a source of great comfort for my beast while I'm away from my ancestral lands." He frowned and then ran a hand roughly through his hair. "It represents a simpler time when I was closer to my family and pack. Back when I got along with my siblings."

I nodded, wondering at what unspoken conflict had wedged between Liam and his pack, but I didn't press him on it. "While Caden's and Marcos' legacies were 'borrowed' from family, yours wasn't. It doesn't sound like you'd be in any trouble if your legacy went missing? Or am I missing something?"

"No, not really," he said.

"Hmm," I hummed, unsure of how this new information helped us. "Okay, what about the maze? Any gut reactions?"

Liam cast his gaze around us. "It's curious to me that the moon is directly overhead while the sun's at two o'clock. It doesn't align with the positions I'd expect."

"We could be in any faery dimension," Marcos added. "The rules here obviously flow differently."

"Agreed," I said. "Anything else about the maze stand out to you?" I asked Liam.

"Not off the top of my head, other than what I've read of in myths. There could be traps. Moving walls. Monsters?" He shrugged.

At the mention of monsters, I giggled nervously. Looking around at the other's sober expressions, I reminded myself that Taneisha no doubt had packed plenty of trouble into this maze for us. We'd only just escaped the man-bird of the netherworld. What fresh hell awaits us in this misty maze?

Which was when I really noticed mist curling up around Emrys' legs, cresting in silent waves as it rolled down the row toward us.

I sidestepped around Liam and walked up to Emrys and Franc, neither of which appeared to have taken notice of the mist. Franc had let go of Emrys, but hovered near his side. I assumed Franc was worried about his behavior. Emrys watched me approach, his expression enigmatic, while all of Franc's focus was on Emrys.

"Uh, guys? Is the mist new, or is it just me?" I asked, pointing down at the roiling fog. As I stepped through it, curls of the mist lapped around my feet. A prickly sensation started in my toes, traveling up my legs. It reminded me of that sensation when a limb fell asleep, except I hadn't lost sensation or movement. I assumed it was magical.

Em didn't respond. Had he realized I'd asked them a question? His gaze remained trained on me, but he was so distant, I wasn't sure he really saw me.

Even though the mist was encroaching, my chaotic energy was strangely quiet. I wasn't about to complain, but

I couldn't help wondering what it meant. Usually my magic reacted during encounters with other magic.

"The fog seems harmless enough," Franc replied. "But we should get moving."

Just then, another gong rang out, again punching me right in the gut. "Oomph!" I doubled over in discomfort. Emrys' hands were tight on my arms, holding me steady on my feet, which was good, because the dizzy sensation returned as the gong reverberated through the air.

"What is up with that?" Franc said under his breath.

"Are you all right?" Liam asked from behind me. Just then, I felt a light touch on my back. That's when everything went sideways.

THE SWEET TASTE OF ALMOST

SERA

Em pulled me in his arms as the sound of fabric ripping filled the air behind me. My breath caught in my throat as I looked into his eyes, captivated by the deep-brown iris flecked with gold which I'd always found so mesmerizing. Emrys was about my height and had a smaller frame than the others in the posse, but he was all lean muscle. Strength I was suddenly all too aware of with my body pressed against the length of his.

By the slight hitch in Em's smile, he knew the effect he had on me. Maybe I should have been irritated by his swagger, but I couldn't help but melt into him.

Keep it together, Sera! I cleared my throat and turned in the demi-god's embrace to see the shredded remains of Liam's clothes floating to the ground as his formidable white wolf stood in his place.

"Now's not the time to wolf out, my man," Marcos said. Caden stood at their side, expression sour and hands on his hips, as if his disapproval alone might correct the situation.

Liam whined, pawed at the ground, and then shook his fluffy mane, causing the mist to scatter around him. I didn't know for sure, but I thought he looked frustrated.

Marcos cocked his head to the side, frowning as the two shifters spoke telepathically. "Liam says he can't change back." Marcos looked up at me. "He thinks touching you forced his shift."

Caden, Marcos, and Liam all stared at me. The maze walls shuddered and groaned, showering us with leaves. Mist continued to swirl around our feet and legs. An ominous weight settled in my stomach.

"Me?" I heard the panicked pitch in my voice. "I know my magic is chaotic, but I did nothing." I tried to go to Liam, but Em held me back. Whether it was to prevent me from going near the wolf or a desire to keep me close, I didn't know.

Emrys' gaze watched Liam, not me. I didn't know what to think of his uncharacteristically quiet, reserved state. When he spoke, it was in a whisper. His voice sounded raw and overused.

"Of all my waking dreams so far, this one is the most curious," Em muttered as if to himself, his breath hot on my neck.

Dreams? Emrys really had lost track of reality in Taneisha's deprivation chamber. Just how far gone was he? I needed to shake him out of it. Quick.

The hedge walls shuddered again, and in the distance, a deep, bellowing roar filled the air. A creature? A man? I couldn't tell. All that was clear was that we weren't alone. Either way, I definitely wanted to go in the other direction.

Em tightened his grip, pulling me into motion. "Run!" he commanded, voice still a whisper.

I let Em pull me along, casting a quick look behind us. I'd hoped to get a glance at the others, but all I could see was a mass of churning greenery cutting through the mists, closing up the path behind us. Was it my imagination, or did I hear something large behind us breaking branches? Adrenaline poured straight into my legs and feet, and soon I was pulling Em, urging him to run even faster. His expression was grim.

"Where's Franc?" I yelled, realizing I'd lost sight of him, too.

Em didn't answer. Instead, we ran on, flanked by the hedge maze on either side. There were no openings, just endless walls boxing us in and forcing our path. Up ahead was a bright wall of mist which grew ever more opaque by the moment. I faltered.

"Don't stop," Em replied.

"You plan to run into the mist?" I asked, breath ragged.

Em cast me a sideways glance. "Choices are to go forward into the mist or wait for the hedge to catch up with us. Here's hoping the mist is a softer landing."

He didn't even have the grace to sound winded, but I couldn't argue with his logic. We pressed on, running headlong into the mist when we reached it. My stride faltered and Em slowed beside me to match my pace as we walked forward through the white, rolling fog. The churning noise of the maze faded, replaced with an oddly familiar background noise I couldn't quite place.

"Can you see anything?" I whispered, my eyes unable to pick anything out of the bright white surrounding us.

"I'm not sure," he answered, but another few steps in the mist dissipated, and he huffed out a dry chuckle. "Of course."

A moment later, I saw it too. Rows of tall hedge had been replaced with shelving packed with bins of coffee and tea. I took a deep breath, my soul soothed by the smells of crema and pastries in the air. I could hear the buzz of activity beyond the closed door. "We're in my shop, Charmed Brews!"

Fingers of mist swirled around the floor and along the walls. If I opened the door, would I find Pepper with a latte in hand?

No. I knew this place wasn't real. Couldn't be real. I'd been so caught up with the posse and Taneisha's challenges, I hadn't slowed down enough to miss home or my shop. An ache filled my chest as I breathed in the familiar scents. How much longer would it take to appease Taneisha before I could return home?

I looked at Em, who was watching me closely, his gaze guarded. Dark. How much longer would I have with him and the rest of the posse? Just how much had Taneisha messed with his head?

"Do you remember this place?" I asked.

Emrys hadn't let go of me, and now he turned and backed me up against a shelf, placing a hand on either side of me. I leaned against a shelf, gripping it with my hands. He was hovering around me like he'd done when Em had first asked for my help, playing out a scene I remembered all too well. "How could I not?" he murmured. Em's gaze raked up my body, lingering on my curves, my neck, and my lips.

Okay, so Em's memory seemed intact, but his usual cocky confidence now had a feral edge to it. Like he was barely holding onto his control. My breathing quickened, and I sucked in my lower lip, rolling it between my teeth.

Perhaps I shouldn't find this version of him even more appealing, but I had to admit that I was fighting a losing battle.

Not just with Emrys.

"I've come back here again and again, Sera," he whispered, the heat of his body sending a shiver through my own. "I'm not sure what else I can say."

Did Em mean he'd revisited this memory while in Taneisha's sensory deprivation tank? Heat blossomed across my cheeks. "Remind me?" I asked, curiosity peaked.

WE AREN'T IN KANSAS ANYMORE

EMRYS

L ike I could deny Sera's plea, spoken from those lush heart-shaped lips as her inviting breasts heaved mere inches away from me? Every time she asked, I gave in. Gave her whatever she asked for. Sometimes she told me to leave, so I'd leave. Sometimes she bantered with me about whether she'd help me and we'd argue back and forth for what felt like hours.

This place, and this scenario, wasn't quite up to Taneisha's prior efforts, but it's not like calling her out would improve my situation, so I just rolled with it. Who cared if the edges of this simulation blurred, giving the background a weird, grainy texture? At least Sera's image was crisp and clear, those brown eyes of hers pulling me into their depths.

I felt the smile creeping across my face as I remembered the best times. The times Sera had demanded my kiss, and I'd been ravenous for her. In those dreams, I'd blazed a trail of kisses over every inch of her flesh. Buried myself inside her until she'd cried out my name. In those moments of bliss, I'd been covered with the sweet jasmine-laced smell of her sweat.

A sparkle of amusement filled Sera's eyes. "What were you going to say, Em?"

I sighed. I wanted to taste her again, but banter it was. Whatever Sera wanted. I sighed and let it all out. My speech felt almost rehearsed by now, but it's not like that mattered. I needed Sera to understand that I knew I'd fucked up. I needed her to forgive me.

"I'm sorry for getting you into this mess with Taneisha. I should never have asked for your help, Sera. It was selfish of me. I knew you owed me, and I hoped your status and power as a mage would give us an edge against the fae. I didn't realize, or even worry about, how much danger you'd be in, and now it's my fault you're stuck in this madhouse with us. It's driving me crazy, not even knowing if you're safe. Screw the legacies. I just want to get out of this dream and get you safely home." I ran a hand through my hair, feeling tension balling into a knot in my stomach. "Assuming I can find you."

Sera's eyes went wide with alarm and took my face in her hands. "I'm right here, Em. I'm fine. We're all fine. And we're all going to get home."

If only what Sera's doppelgänger said was true, but I'd been through all of this before. So many times. How long had I been in Taneisha's special version of hell? There was no way for me to know. The hours and days had blended together. Had I even slept? I couldn't recall. I'd lived and breathed this surreal landscape of disappointment for far too long. I wasn't even sure my memories of the time before were correct.

Enough wallowing.

I tucked Sera's hair behind her ear, loving the silky feel of it against my fingers. Loving the feel of her hands on me. These visions of Sera were the best dreams. "If anything happens to you, I swear I'll never forgive myself. I hope one day you can forgive me."

Her brow furrowed. Sera leaned forward and kissed me on the cheek. "I'm a big girl, Em. I knew helping you against a fae was a bad idea, yet I did it anyway."

Her fingers threaded through the hair at my nape, pulling me into a near-electric kiss that swept me away. I let myself fall into her embrace, pushing Sera back against the shelf, greedy for her heat. I knew this delusion might all fade away at any moment, but at this moment, I could almost believe Sera was real. When she bit my lower lip with her teeth, I sucked in a breath. She hadn't done that before.

I debated pushing this encounter in a new direction. How much room to play would I have in this dream?

"What's going on inside that head of yours?" she whispered into my ear.

I chuckled. "I'm just reminiscing over our prior liaisons and curious where this one will take us."

"Sounds like this scene has been a recurring theme?"

I was a little taken aback at her question, because it seemed out of character for the dream, but I definitely liked where this dream was headed. "Most definitely. We've tried so many things. So many variations on a theme. I'm curious what will manifest this time."

Sera pulled back, a wicked look in her eyes under an arched brow. "Hmm. Is there anything I've been unwilling to do in these dreams of yours?"

She'd always been direct, but this Sera was more flirty

than I remembered, and I loved it. I opened my mouth to answer, but hesitated, suddenly anxious to disclose to this version of Sera what I'd been up to with all the prior versions of her.

Before I'd decided, Franc strode right through the far wall of the 'pantry' and rushed up to us. This gave me pause. It was unusual for elements of these visions to disobey the laws of physics, but perhaps this was a new twist in Taneisha's ruse?

"There you are," Franc said, seemingly oblivious to the obvious intimacy of the moment. "Something's coming." He looked back and forth between us, as if this announcement should have some meaning.

"Something...like what? What did you see?" Sera asked, her lips pinker and plumper from our kisses, but her focus was now entirely on the new potential threat. Damn Franc's interruption.

Franc reached out, resting his hand on Sera's shoulder. Comforting? Proprietary? Definitely with the ease of someone who'd done so a fair amount. The nerve of him, considering that she was here with me now. In my arms. Her cheeks flushed from my kisses.

When she smiled up at Franc with affection in her gaze, I took a step back. I remembered all too well, bursting in on Sera and the others back at the shed. Images flashed through my mind. Everyone caught up in their passions, lost to pleasure. Everyone except me. What else might have happened between the posse and Sera while I've been gone? It wasn't their fault. My choice to steal, knowing it would anger Taneisha, had been my own.

I didn't look forward to finding out. I wasn't usually the jealous type, but Sera's inclusion on this trip had been my choice. Mine. It wasn't fair they had excluded me. I shook my head. I was being ridiculous. It's not like this was real. Until I got out of Taneisha's deprivation chamber, I just needed to keep my shit together.

It'd also be great if I could stop torturing myself about being left out of the action. Me imagining Franc intruding on my moment with Sera was just my way of making myself miserable.

Franc snapped his fingers in front of my face, and I glared up at him. "I'm not sure, but it's something large. We need to go."

That's when I heard something approaching at the far end of the room near the door leading to Sera's shop. Or, I supposed, somewhere else. It just sounded large, with heavy footfalls heralding its approach. The handle rattled a moment later. None of us needed more encouragement.

"This way," Franc said, moving in the direction he'd come, heading straight for the back wall.

Sera needed no encouragement. We grabbed our bags, which we'd dropped to the floor earlier, and rushed to follow Franc. I heard a creaking sound behind us and glanced back in time to see the door open, a large, dark-skinned hand on the handle. The next moment I was through the wall, once again finding myself jogging down the maze with a wall of mist at our backs.

"Have you seen the others?" Sera asked Franc.

"No," Franc replied. "I'm guessing you didn't either, holed up in that memory back there."

Memory? What were they talking about?

We continued to jog along. The rows were wide enough for us to run side by side, so I had no problem seeing the flush that crept over Sera's cheeks.

"We got distracted," she huffed out. "Did you get stuck in a memory pocket, too?"

Franc frowned, but nodded. "I landed in one, but escaped pretty quickly."

"What was it?" I gasped, slowing down into a fast walk. The others followed my lead, with Franc glancing backwards.

"I found myself back on my grandfather's land in Naxos, surrounded by goats. I knew it couldn't be real, so I found my way out and searched for you two. Figured you couldn't be that far away, since you were only a few steps behind me."

"Goats? Yeah, I would have run from them too." Sera looked to Franc, then me, then back to Franc again. "I don't think Em understands this is the real world. Do you, Em?"

I hesitated and fell behind, unsure of how to answer.

"Let's head this way," Franc interrupted, leading us on a turn to the right, which led down another long row. At least the visuals were clear again, no longer grainy like an old television. Perhaps Taneisha had corrected whatever the prior issue was? "Well, Em? Have you figured out this is real yet?"

What? I walked faster to keep up with them. This was entirely new, not something that had happened in the visions Taneisha had sent me over and over. Sure, I'd seen plenty of Sera and Franc, but never had they been aware of the illusion. They were more like characters in my own personal play.

My head spun, and I stopped. They stopped alongside me, although Franc glanced behind us anxiously. "The storage room at Charmed Brews, the one Sera and I were just in. You're saying that was fake?"

"Yes, Em. It was you and me in that pantry together. The maze is quite real, although it appears able to construct illusions." Sera nodded, adjusting her pack on her shoulders.

I thought about what I'd admitted to Sera in the pantry, alluding to all the times we'd done more than simply kiss in my fantasies. When I thought of what else I'd considered sharing with her, I felt myself rock back on the soles of my feet. But if she'd been offended, it didn't show. That was assuming this was real, and not just some new twist on a delusional theme from Taneisha.

I needed time to make sense of all this. Maybe if I pretended I was behaving normally, these versions of Sera and Franc would as well?

"Okay. Well, I'm glad to be back in the real world, or whatever this place is." I hitched a smile, hoping for them to buy my act, and Sera smiled back reassuringly, but she still furrowed her brow with concern.

"We should keep moving," she said. She led us off at a fast walking pace in the opposite direction from where the pantry room had been located.

Just like that, we'd all officially moved on. Except all I wanted was another taste of her lips, but that wasn't likely to happen soon. I also figured they'd both be keeping an eye on me, which was fine, because I'd be watching them, too.

"We need to be very careful," Franc added. "Since we have no idea when it'll happen again, or why. I believe the illusions are connected to the mists, but time will tell."

"Agreed," Sera replied. "Hopefully, the mist is a consistent signal. Any ideas on how we find the others?"

"So eager to get back to them?" The words slipped out before my filter kicked in, and it did not surprise me when Sera narrowed her gaze at me.

"Of course I am. We're stuck here in this maze until we find Liam's legacy, which I assume will be easier to do with all of us working together. Don't you want that too?"

I knew the right answer was yes, so why was I digging in my proverbial emotional heels? I shook my head. On the outside chance this maze was real and Liam's legacy was on the line, I needed to pull my head out of my ass and get back in the game real quick.

"Sure, we need to find them, but maybe this is actually a good thing. Let's split into two groups. We can cover more territory and maybe even find his legacy faster."

"I agree," Franc said. "I think it's foolhardy to attempt finding them in this maze when we don't even know where we are."

Sera shrugged. "Maybe you're both right, but I don't have to like it."

"What's our move?" I asked. I wasn't usually the one asking. Usually I was the one driving the action, but there was nothing typical about this journey.

"For the time being," Franc replied, "We need to push forward and see if we can find Liam's moonstone wolf's head while avoiding whatever that creature was back there."

"Game strategy dictates we follow the right-hand rule," Sera added. When we both frowned at her, she continued. "It's where you keep your right hand on the maze wall and keep it there until you find the center or the exit."

"Lead on, princess," Franc replied. There was a flash of something between them. Defiance in Sera's eyes and a familiar ease on Franc's part.

I held my tongue, knowing fighting the illusion was a lost cause. I was desperate to know what all had happened since I'd been gone, but I had no proof that this was anything other than another trick. Only time would tell.

THE FAE'S PROMISE

LIAM

An otherworldly fog filled the air, burning at my sensitive muzzle and clouding my keen vision. I padded forward, the grassy ground soft under my paws as I looked for Sera and the others.

When the mist cleared, Sera emerged, but Em and Franc were nowhere to be found. The fog formed an opaque wall behind her.

"We've got to find them," Caden said. He was carrying my bag, but his focus was on the mist before us.

I moved between Caden and the mist, issuing a low growl of warning. Like hell I was going to let anyone back into that mist. I sniffed Sera, who stood there rubbing her temples. She smelled off. I assumed that was likely either remnants of the mist clinging to her or my nose being wonky from the acrid mist.

Another roar barreled out through the wall of mist. The scent of an unfamiliar creature raised my hackles. A low growl erupted from my throat as I moved forward between whatever was coming and Sera. Whatever it was, it'd have to go through me to get to her.

"The demi-gods can handle themselves." Marcos rushed to Sera, who was staring into space as she shivered. "C'mon, we have to move quickly," he said, pulling Sera close. "We need to get some distance between us and whatever this is."

I barked my assent. *Let's go. Now.*

"Liam's in agreement," Marcos said, pulling an unusually pliant Sera along with him.

Our little mage remained quiet, which was enough to set off alarm bells in my mind. What had the mist, or the maze, done to her? It reaffirmed my instinct to not search for Em and Franc, at least not until Sera recovered. Of all of us, I had faith those two demi-gods could handle whatever the maze threw at them. I followed the others, glancing back every few steps to check that the mist wasn't getting any closer.

Caden huffed, but relented, jogging to catch up with Marco and Sera, and I trotted along behind them. "Fine, but I am not okay with this decision. What do you think, Sera? Should we go back after them?"

Sera leaned heavily on Marcos, his arm wrapped around her waist. He'd been limping more, favoring his injured leg from the wraith attack in the Netherworld, but that hadn't stopped him from practically carrying Sera. Had he hurt himself further during our encounter with the fog?

"I really don't want to go back into the mist," she replied, her expression verging on panic. At least she was more steady on her feet. The mist was clearing as we moved further away, and although I could still scent the creature on the breeze, the sounds seemed to fade with our distance from the wall of fog.

We reached the end of the row and came to a hard stop, our options either to the left or right. We were beyond the curling mists, but stuck within the maze with no clear path forward and no hints about which option was better.

"What's your wolf's nose say?" Marcos asked.

I ran to the left, then the right, scenting out our options. My snout was full of grasses, dirt, and other plants, but nothing distinguished the options. Turned to Marcos and shook my head. *"I can't tell any difference."*

"He says there's no clear better path," Marcos explained to Sera and Caden. Marcos was still limping, which made them a slow pair. "Well, it's your legacy we're after. You pick, just do it quickly."

I could have pointed out that the wrong decision might lead us back into danger, but what would have been the point? We each knew there were risks, otherwise Taneisha wouldn't have sent us here. I took a last look down each row, spying a turn not far down the left path, and padded off in that direction.

The others followed in silence, caution no doubt being on the top of all our minds. I led us down a series of turns intended to put some space between us and the beast in the mists, led purely by my wolf's sense of direction and scent.

"Hold up," Caden said, coming to a stop. "We've got some distance between us and whatever that was, but I don't want to get too far from the others, either. What's our plan?"

I circled around them, coming to stand next to Sera,

who reached down and scratched me between the ears. She still didn't seem quite herself, but at least she seemed more alert again. No doubt the fog had messed with her mind. I couldn't tell if our prior contact had been what forced me to shift, or the fog. Maybe a mixture of both? Whichever, nothing happened when she touched me now.

"We need to look around for clues while avoiding whatever's following us. I can't believe it'd turn out well if we ran into it," I said to Marcos.

Marcos relayed my thoughts to the others as he rubbed his leg, grimacing as he applied pressure. "Are you able to shift back yet? It'd be easier to strategize if I wasn't translating for you."

I hadn't tried to shift since leaving the fog, intent on using my wolf's nose to the advantage. But Marcos had a point. I took a few steps away and set my intention. This time, the shift worked, with nothing blocking me. Without knowing for sure what had caused it, how could I know if a forced shift might happen again?

"Welcome back to the land of the bipeds," Caden said, holding out my backpack. "Here's your shit."

I arched a brow at him, but Caden's mood was dark. "Thanks for carrying it," I said, to which Caden frowned. I searched through my bag and found some clothes, pulling them on as I found them.

"No biggie, I suppose," Caden said. Which was exactly what a person said when it was a big deal. He ran a hand through his raven hair, pulling it back from his icy blue eyes, as he eyed the maze walls with suspicion. "I'm not even sure what direction we're supposed to take. Do we just keep walking and hope we find the others through pure luck?"

"Do you have a better idea?" I asked.

Caden's expression soured. "All I'm saying is we need a plan. Em and Franc are the shoot from the hip pair. You're the deliberative planners."

"Deliberative?" Marcos laughed. "Have I mentioned how much I like this version of you?" Marcos asked, and Caden's expression softened at the compliment. "I think we need to look around and see what clues we can find. What we find will drive our plan." He glanced at Sera, brows furrowing. "You've been strangely quiet, and you're our game strategist. What say you, mage? Any clever strategies for mazes in that clever mind of yours?"

"Not really," she began, her gaze wandering back and forth between the three of us.

"You're not sure?" I asked her. Sera looked at me and shrugged. Shrugged!

I tensed and glanced at Marcos, who stood near her, his arms now crossed. *"Does our normally opinionated little mage seem off to you?"*

"Sure, but everything seems a bit off here."

"Especially Sera."

"Agreed."

Caden sighed. "You're both being rude."

"Me?" Sera asked, eyes wide.

The misunderstanding could have been cute, but it set my teeth on edge. Sera seemed unusually slow and out of it. Just how badly had the fog messed with her?

"No, them." Caden pointed at Marcos and me, drawing lines between us in the air. "The point of you being in your human skin was to have us all talking out loud. To each other. Now, out with it."

"Liam's worried about Sera," Marcos said.

"Me?" Sera asked. This time her gaze traveled back and forth between Marcos and me, her brow furrowed with confusion. I watched her closely, eager for her reaction, but Sera's expression remained curiously unemotional.

A chill ran over my skin at the inherent wrongness of her reaction.

"Why couldn't you have said that out loud?" Caden asked.

"I'm fine, guys," Sera replied, waving a hand in front of her as if that would brush away our concerns. "And l think Marcos' idea of looking around for clues is great, but I'm worried about his leg. Is it hurting more?"

"Deflection, much?" I asked Marcos.

"Glad to hear it's not just me wondering what's gotten into her," he replied.

Marcos nodded. "Yeah, but my leg can wait. We've got bigger things to worry about."

"That's unusual for you," Sera replied. She wasn't wrong. Shifters healed quickly and the injury to Marcos' leg from the wraith attack had been lingering for days now. "I'm worried being here in the maze might have made it worse. Show us."

"When you put it like that, I want to have a look, too," Caden chimed in, his voice full of concern.

"Look, fine, just so we can move past this," Marcos replied. He bent down into a squat and pulled up his left pant leg, revealing a deep, blackened bruise running up the length of his shin and wrapping back and around his calf.

A beat of silence passed.

I remembered how the injury had looked fresh, and this was no improvement. The shadowy bruise contrasted starkly against the bronzed hue of Marcos' dark sand skin tone. I'd seen Marcos scrap plenty over the years, and I remembered him weathering his fair share of scuffs and bruises. Never had he bruised this badly. I didn't doubt all of us knew there was something seriously wrong with Marcos' leg.

"Shit, man." Caden blew out a low whistle. "That's worse. Way worse."

"I guess I should have been paying more attention," Marcos replied.

"We've been plenty distracted and you've always been one to power through," I said. "For better or, in this case, worse. What have you tried?"

"Let me look," Sera said, interrupting Marcos' reply. She dropped onto her knees in front of Marcos with a look of wide-eyed fascination. She reached out and placed her hand against the bruise.

Both she and Marcos jolted as if a wave of electricity had hit them both. Was this anything like when she'd touched me after the fog? Marcos didn't shift, but his expression grew pained as he bared his teeth, grinding them together.

"Sera, stop!" I said, hearing the panic in my voice. She didn't respond, her eyes now closed, her attention lost to us.

"Should we separate them?" Caden asked. We'd both stepped forward, hovering near Marcos and Sera.

I opened my mouth to respond, but as I watched Marcos' leg, I forgot what I was about to say. The inky blackness moved and swirled against his skin, rolling into mounds and tendrils.

Caden and I shared a panicked glance.

That blackness looked just like a wraith.

Marcos cried out in pain as the darkness pulled away from his flesh and wrapped itself around Sera's arm. She fell back on her ass, cradling her blackened arm. Marcos leaned back, dazed, staring at Sera.

"Tell me that wasn't a wraith," I said to Caden.

He held up his hands. "It's not possible. Some sort of residual ephemera?"

Whatever that meant, but this was no time to debate the creatures of the Netherworld. This situation had gone off the rails, and I could think of only one thing to do.

"Taneisha, Taneisha, Taneisha!" I yelled.

The fae arrived a moment later dressed in a sheath dress of pale green moss. Had she been expecting our summons?

"Giving up so soon?" Taneisha pouted blood-red lips, but there was a glint of triumph in her eyes.

"I'm not, but Sera's ill," I said. "You promised to remove any of us who became injured. Please take her with you and heal her."

"Is she?" Taneisha looked down at Sera, and then back at me, her nose wrinkled up like she'd smelled something nasty. "What's that goo?"

"Residual wraith components?" Caden said, his tone more query than answer.

Sera opened her eyes, and Marcos backed away from her and stood, his movements suddenly wary. A tarry blackness covered her arm, and when she stood and turned to us, we could see her eyes were fully black.

Taneisha shuddered. Caden stood dumbfounded.

How were we going to fix this? I had to hope the fae would have an answer.

"Sera said you'd agreed to remove us from the maze and heal us. Prevent anything that happens here from causing permanent damage," I said to the fae. "Whatever this is, it's clearly a medical crisis."

Taneisha raised a finger. "Yes, that's correct. I didn't expect this." She tapped her finger against her lips. "I agree. It's not at all natural."

I let out a breath I didn't realize I'd been holding. "So you can fix this?"

Taneisha pursed her lips and arched a brow. "I will take Sera with me if she asks to go."

What new fae trickery was this?

"And heal her?" Marcos asked, coming to stand near me.

Taneisha rolled her eyes. "Yes, of course I'd heal her. I'm no monster."

The black-eyed Sera watched us, but I couldn't get a read on her. Could it be the wraith taint on her? Did she even understand what was going on?

"Sera, tell Taneisha you want to go with her. Leave the maze," I urged.

Sera smiled a wry smile and took a step backward. "This has been fun, boys."

"Ask her to take you," Caden pleaded. "The fae will help you."

"Okay," Sera replied, but took another step back, pressing herself against the hedge wall behind her. "I want to go with you, Taneisha. I want to leave the maze."

Taneisha's expression grew stormy. "I will do no such thing," she spat out.

"But you swore..." I started, frustrated past the point of

civility with Taneisha, but she held up a hand to cut me off, a glare of warning in her brown eyes.

"Wolf, when Sera asks, I will take her. Until then, I am not honor bound."

"What the hells!" Caden exclaimed. "Didn't she just do that?"

Taneisha didn't answer. Marcos, Caden, and I shared a look. The fae couldn't lie. Which meant...

The black-eyed Sera giggled. "I suppose the gig, as they say, is up." Sera blew the three of us kisses, one after the other. "It's been fun, boys! Oh, and thanks for the boost." The black-eyed Sera winked and then stepped backward through the hedge in a puff of blackened mist.

"What the hell just happened?" Caden huffed out.

Marcos let out a low growl. "That wasn't our Sera. It was some maze trickery."

"Wasn't just the maze," Marcos added. "That false Sera might have started off as a maze trick, but with the wraith, she's now something altogether different."

My wolf howled within my chest, straining to break free. Urging me to run, to find Sera, to know that she was safe.

"Where is she?" I demand from Taneisha, hearing the edge of my wolf's hunger in my tone.

"Safe enough that she's not calling for me," she laughed. "Now, if you don't mind, I must be off. Happy hunting."

FUMBLING THROUGH THE MISTS

EMRYS

We walked and walked, row after row, always following the hedge on our right as Sera had suggested. I'd fallen behind Sera and Franc, preferring to watch them talk like I was watching some sort of movie. Their body language, more than their words, spoke of how close they'd become. The lingering glances. The familiar, casual touches. The easy way the cadence of their conversation flowed from topic to topic.

I wanted to believe this wasn't one of the fae's tricks, but it was hard to trust myself to know the difference. I wanted to trust Franc and Sera, but that meant buying into this maze place being real.

I'd be no fool for Taneisha. Sera? Anytime.

Sera glanced back at me over her shoulder. "What do you think, Em?"

"Huh?" I asked. I suppose I should have been paying more attention, but after so long entertaining myself with my own thoughts, it was difficult to keep my focus on the present. I'd rather wax poetic on the curve of Sera's jeans, but I still had enough wits about me to know that would cross the bounds of acceptable social behavior.

Assuming this was real, which I dared to hope it was.

Franc's smile felt forced, his eyes full of concern. "You're welcome to join in whenever you want. I'd love hearing your perspective on the maze's illusions."

I rolled my eyes. "Perspective? What perspective is there beyond another of Taneisha's games?"

Franc opened his mouth to reply, but Sera laid a hand on his arm, shooting him a pointed glance. To my surprise, Franc held his tongue. Sera was a mage, but Franc listening to her was pure witchery. But was that evidence of this present moment being an illusion, or real? Only time would tell.

"You look pretty lost in your thoughts," Sera said. "Mind sharing with the rest of us?"

I couldn't help myself. I flashed what I hoped was still my winning smile at her. "You're the game expert here, mage. How do you see this maze's purpose?"

Her slight smile wasn't the effect I'd been hoping for, but the way her face lit up delighted me. "Well, mazes exist to be solved. There's usually a prize, which we have in Liam's legacy. Escaping can also be the goal, but I could argue that our escape is via the prize, since we can't leave without it."

"That's pretty clear," I said.

She nodded. "True, but it bears saying. Mazes can also be metaphorical journeys into the choices we each face in life, or deeper understandings of our own psyches."

Franc ran his hand along the leaves of the hedge wall. "This doesn't feel metaphorical."

Sera chuckled. "Agreed, but I suspect the illusions

might function to revisit or test our choices. Thus, the memory pockets we experienced. We also don't know if this maze is Taneisha's creation or something she found and co-opted for her use. And while this maze is physical, it may also have dynamic elements."

Franc stopped. "You think it could have moving parts?"

"Dynamic mazes are common in lore. But that isn't what worries me."

"Then what worries you?" I asked. "You know we'll protect you."

The grin she flashed me this time was wholehearted. "I do, Em. Although I'm less worried about us than about the others. It might just be my overactive imagination, but I'm worried they're in trouble." She swept her hair out of her face, tucking it behind her ear. Suddenly, I wanted nothing more than to brand a line of kisses along her neck, banishing her concerns about the others. "I'm worried this maze might have divided us on purpose," she whispered.

"Sounds like you got pretty close to the others while Taneisha had me locked up," I said, the words pouring out of me before I could tap my mental brakes.

The smile washed right off of Sera's face, replaced with a fiery glint in her eyes. "We crossed the Netherworld together. Without you, only because you ignored the fae's rules and got yourself in trouble. Now you're jealous you missed out on the experience?"

Any person in their right mind would know not to test a mage's temper, but I'd never excelled at holding back my emotions. Instead, I stepped closer to her. Franc came close enough to stop me, but didn't.

"What did I miss out on?"

Sera crossed her arms, her brow arched high. "Are you

asking about how far we walked or how many creatures of the underworld we fought off?"

I took a deep breath, and I swore I could smell the flare of her temper singe the surrounding air. I ran a hand through my hair. "You know what I mean," I muttered.

"I don't think I do, Em. Out with it, golden boy."

I groaned. Was this even real? Did anything I do even matter in this place? I sighed. I'd never been good at sitting on my curiosity. My angst was real, even if this place wasn't.

It was Franc's turn to arch a brow my way, but I recognized that bemused smile curling his lips. He was enjoying the show.

Let him.

"Look, I'm no shifter, so I can't scent others on you, but I can sense you've all grown closer. The posse seem more protective of you, too."

"We've been through a lot in a short time together," Sera replied.

"Liam insisted you had mating marks, and I know how driven shifters can be to claim their mates. So, are you one of theirs now?"

She frowned. "I belong to no one. I'm my own person."

So why didn't I believe her?

Franc, hand over his mouth, let out a soft cough. "Sorry to interrupt." He leaned close to Sera, tucked her hair behind her ear, and then leaned in. When he spoke, it was in a breathy whisper. "I have to say, I certainly admired how you asserted your independence back in that shower."

"Thanks?" Sera's cheeks flushed crimson. "They have not claimed me. Mated. Or whatever," she stammered.

Franc took a step back and shook his head. "Of course not. You've demonstrated you're perfectly capable of claiming who you want, when you want."

My stomach sank as Franc confirmed my fears. Off in Taneisha's void, I'd missed out on more than just helping Caden retrieve his legacy. The posse and Sera had moved on without me. By the gist of it, together.

"I haven't claimed the posse as my mates!" she exclaimed. "I'm not looking for that."

"Never said you had," Franc replied, but by his smug smile I knew he'd gotten the rise out of Sera that he'd been looking for. As a god of revelry, Franc felt almost pathologically compelled to point out when people denied their urges. "But that hasn't stopped you from taking what you wanted, and I certainly have heard no one complaining."

She stared at him for a moment, and then let out a long breath. "You're impossible," Sera said. "Which I know you know."

Franc grinned at her, then at me. "I'll admit I have my charms."

Franc and I usually played wingman for each other with women. Sometimes with the same woman, and sometimes more. Now he was playing mediator and taking Sera's side over mine? My instinct was to snap back at Franc, but his demeanor had me second-guessing myself, so I held my tongue. I wasn't truly angry at either of them. Hurt? Definitely, but I had only myself to blame for feeling left out on my chance with Sera.

Enough talking. Either this was an illusion, and I'd become an expert at torturing myself or it was real and I'd missed my opportunity to woo Sera as my own. It sounded like she had exactly what she wanted. "We should keep moving," I said, turning and walking around them both.

Sera caught me by the arm. "You weren't gone that long, Em. You're back now and things will feel like they're back to normal before you know it."

She was right. I was back now, but well behind in winning Sera's affections. "You're right. I'm sorry. I should have been there for you. All of you."

"I don't think I've ever seen you more sincere," she said, cupping a hand along my jaw. "It looks good on you. Thank you."

I shot Sera a half-hearted smile, which she returned with enthusiasm. We continued down the row, Sera and I walking side by side, Franc trailing along behind us.

We'd only gone a few paces when I did a double-take and backed up a few paces, turning and facing the hedge wall on our right.

"What's wrong?" Sera asked.

I pointed. "We missed a turn to the right."

Sera and Franc shared a worried glance. "What do you mean, we missed a turn? There's nothing but a hedge wall there," Franc said.

I inspected the hedge wall, which to my eyes had a grainy appearance. It stood out from the typical regularity of the surrounding hedge, reminding me of the illusory room Sera and I had been stuck in before. In my gut, I knew this had to be an illusion, too.

"You don't see the difference in the wall here?" I asked them, pointing to the section which looked irregular. No, that wasn't quite right. Besides appearing grainy, there was a repetition to the image that wasn't quite natural to me.

Franc cleared his throat behind me to get my attention,

but I ignored him. "It looks about the same as the rest," he said.

"Are you guys messing with me? You really notice nothing different here?" I asked.

"I don't," Sera replied. "But it might be something you can see that we can't. Can you show us?"

Either I was right, or I was about to solidify my impression of having gone off the deep end with them. Doubt churned in my gut, but I stepped forward, my hands reaching out before me, intent on walking directly into the hedge of illusion.

The moment that my fingertips met the leafy hedge, the illusion faded in a puff of grayish fog, revealing a short opening leading to a path which ran parallel to the one we'd been following. I took a half step back, wary of the magical impacts the fog had on us previously. Luckily, this time, the mist didn't last long, wafting away on the breeze within seconds.

Franc clapped me on the shoulder. "Point to Em and his eagle eyes. That's a neat trick."

"It is!" Sera's smile warmed more than just my heart. "We would have missed this right turn without you catching it. Is this the first time you've noticed an illusion like that?" Sera asked.

I nodded, running a hand around the back of my neck. "This is the first time I've noticed one since we stumbled into your fake pantry room."

When I glanced up at Sera to see her reaction, I noticed the slow hint of a smile curling her lips. At least I wasn't the only one thinking back on those moments fondly. Perhaps I still had a shot after all?

"Let's check it out," Franc said, striding boldly forward

through the opening.

Sera and I followed him, looking back and forth down the hedgerow. At first glance, it appeared the same as the rest of the maze.

Until it didn't.

Far down the row to our left, dark shadows appeared, expanding and swirling, obscuring the sunny space. A deep, lowing sound followed a moment later.

"I've got a bad, familiar feeling right about now," Franc said under his breath.

"That's definitely the same rumble we heard before," Sera added. "When we got separated from the others."

A moment later, an enormous form emerged from the shadows and lumbered towards us. I recognized it, despite never having seen one of the rare creatures in the flesh. The minotaur swung his massive head from side to side, his horns brushing against the hedge as he moved. I guessed his height was over seven or maybe eight feet tall. His hands fisted as his large, chestnut brown eyes focused on us.

No warm, fuzzy vibes here. But why the hell would a minotaur be wearing khakis? Sure, they were frayed and raggedy, but khakis didn't fit any typical monster vibe.

"We need to go. C'mon!" Franc yelled, breaking us out of our stupor. Sera and I turned and ran, Franc close on our heels.

"I just remembered another type of maze I didn't mention before," Sera gasped.

"What?" I asked.

"Sometimes mazes are houses for monsters," she replied. "As in their hunting grounds."

I ran faster.

CORNERED

I probably, definitely, shouldn't have said that bit about mazes being monster hunting grounds, but I have a habit of blurting things out when my anxiety got to me.

The sound of the minotaur stomping behind us wasn't helping anything. Em ran beside me, easily keeping to my pace. No doubt he and Franc could have gone faster, yet they stayed by my side. Ironically, if the minotaur caught up, I was the one with the mage abilities to defend us. Assuming my magic would behave itself. I knew the demigods were both more resilient than me, especially Em with his divine gift of resurrection from Isis, but I didn't think either of them could charm their way out of that behemoth of muscle bearing down on us.

At least Em seemed to be shaking off his confusion. I couldn't tell if he was certain that he was in the real world yet, but at least he was taking things seriously. I knew I couldn't let Em out of my sight until I was certain he'd returned to us mentally, and I sincerely doubted Franc would either. The last thing we needed was him wandering off on his own in this state.

The minotaur rumbled and lowed behind us, and I felt the reverberations in the air. Was he any closer? I feared to look back.

Damn Taneisha and her games. I made a mental note to give her an even larger piece of my mind the next time she showed up.

Unexpectedly, the row took a turn to the right and opened up into a wide, open space. Someone had arranged roses and statues symmetrically around a central fountain, like a formal garden attached to a manor house or castle. It looked so pretty, quaint, and well maintained. Not at all like a realm home to wild monsters.

No, for the proper ambiance, the garden should have been filled with overgrown wild brambles and crumbling statues. Not these delicate carvings of feminine wood nymphs and muscular warriors.

I heard the beast round the corner behind us, stomping its way into the glen. He shook his weighty head from side to side, stomping his hooves and huffing noisily. His blowing was so loud, I half expected smoke to erupt from his nostrils.

I scanned the walls, but there were only two exits, both on the same wall, maybe fifty feet apart. The minotaur stood at the one on the left, and we'd have to cross his path to make it to the other opening.

He'd cornered us, and the minotaur appeared ready to rumble.

I grabbed Em's arm, whose attention was fixed on the hedge wall behind us. Somehow, he was the calmest out of the three of us. Was this new cool composure a side effect of the trials Taneisha had put him through?

"Please tell me you see another hidden passageway nearby?"

Em's smile was strained. "No, but I'm still looking. Don't worry. There's a trick to this game, and we'll figure it out."

I took a deep breath and blew it out. Em was right. We'd figure something out.

The minotaur started pacing back and forth, snorting and waving his arms. He continued to block both of the potential exit routes from us. Franc moved between us and the minotaur, brandishing one of the camping knives in his hand. I moved to stand next to him. I focused my will, hoping to feel my magic build, but nothing seemed to happen.

Just like old times.

"I doubt your little blade will do much against that hulk," I muttered. "Have you even fought with a knife before?"

Franc gave a quick shake of his head. "You know I'm a lover, not a fighter, but I will not stand here doing nothing when that creature attacks us. If you're planning on zapping him, do it sooner than later."

I tucked my hair behind my ear. "My magic fizzled out earlier when we arrived, and I'm worried it might not deliver now. I'd hate to attempt walloping that beast just to have my magic crap out. I might just poke it and piss it off."

"You did accidentally zap Liam earlier, sure, but you've shown us time and time again the power of your magic."

He tilted his head to the side. "Perhaps you need to have a little more faith in yourself?"

Those were kind words, but I knew my history with my magic. Recent events were a fluke, not the norm. "I hear you, but I'm telling you my magic is not responding right now."

"Sorry to hear it. You got any better ideas than our knives, because it feels like we're running low on options?"

I wracked my brain as I ranted out loud. "Taneisha gave us plenty of supplies, but no weapons beyond the utility knives. She billed this challenge as a maze to be solved. I figured we were here to hunt a lost legacy, not a mythical beast."

"Why not both?" Franc said, a sardonic grin curling his mouth. "Said none of us ever."

A glowering Em rejoined us, running his fingers back through his dark, curly hair, which had gotten wild from the run. He'd been so quiet, I wondered when, or if, the cocky playboy might return. Despite myself, I missed his surly self-confidence. A stray lock hung over his eyes, and I wanted to brush it out of his face and help him set it to rights, but now was not the time.

"I couldn't locate any hidden exits. The minotaur chased us here, so why isn't he attacking us now?" Em asked. "And why the hell is he dressed like that?"

"What do you mean? Like what?" The minotaur had little on except for a kilt-like loincloth hanging from his hips.

I didn't get an answer because at that moment, familiar faces appeared at the other opening in the hedge. Liam, Caden, and Marcos could see us, but they couldn't see the Minotaur pacing and loudly raving mere feet from where they stood. When I realized what was going to happen next, my heart skipped a beat. I opened my mouth to scream something, anything, to stop them and send them back, but it was too late.

Liam took off at a run across the glen in our direction, Caden and Marcos following close behind him. The minotaur turned toward them and bellowed before lowering his head and charging.

Marcos and Liam ran even faster. Caden, paler than a ghost from the Netherworld, stumbled and then tripped, falling face first into a flower bed. I held up my hands, not to cast a spell, but to point and alert Liam, whose gaze hadn't left me since he'd stepped into the glen. He glanced back at where I was pointing and stopped short, gracefully pivoting and falling into a crouch behind a short bush as he watched the beast bearing down on Caden. Marcos followed his cue. Even from this distance, I could see them wordlessly gesturing back and forth.

"Hey! Bull!" Franc hollered. "Over here!"

If the creature heard Franc, he didn't show it. Em and I joined in the shouting, my heart beating at a gallop. The minotaur continued his relentless charge, unaware that the guys were no longer in his direct path. Although he wasn't moving quickly, I knew that much mass would flatten whatever it hit.

Caden recovered and poked his head up. One glance back over his shoulder was all it took to fuel his scramble forward, straight under a nearby hydrangea bush. Pompoms of blush-tinged petals swayed and banged together above him, creating a bubblegum rain declaring his path toward Liam and Marcos.

Would the minotaur notice Caden's movement off to

his right? A few more barreling steps proved the beast was intent on his path, and I let out a breath I didn't realize I'd been holding. Caden had a real chance to get away.

I'd been paying so much attention to the minotaur and the posse, I almost didn't notice the black miasma emerging from the hedge opening. The same one the guys had just arrived through a few moments ago. The dark cloud coalesced into a human shape.

My shape, but wrong. Black eyes. Black nails raised to attack. It even bared blackened teeth in a wild, angry snarl.

The minotaur hit it going full speed, spearing the newly formed body with his massive horns. The beast's speed carried them forward, inevitable as a freight train.

An additional threat should have shocked me, but it didn't. I was pissed because it looked like me, but me as some sort of dark phantasm. "What the fuck is that?"

"Definitely not you," Franc replied. "Another trick of Taneisha's, no doubt."

"What do you want to do?" Em asked.

"We wait and see who wins," I answered, waving Marcos, Liam, and Caden over to our spot on the far side of the garden from the fighting monsters. "Then we only have to fight the victor."

CONFESSIONS AND COMPLICATIONS

LIAM

The minotaur plowed into wraith-Sera at full bore, sending them tumbling head over tail over miasma. The wraith shrieked. The minotaur roared. Marcos and I stayed low as they tumbled past, a flurry of movement and grunts.

My wolf howled inside my chest. I needed to get to Sera. Hold her. Reassure myself that she was okay. That she was mine.

A flower-petal and dirt covered Caden reached us a few moments later. "What'd I miss?"

"The wraith-Sera followed us here," Marcos explained in a whisper. "We need to fall back while they're occupied."

"Ready?" I asked Caden. He scrambled up into a squat and gave us a nod. We rose and left one after the other, Caden first and with Marcos in the rear.

I couldn't seem to run fast enough to reach the others. To reach Sera. The glen wasn't that big, but after a day spent cornered in by hedgerows, this open space felt expansive.

When I reached the others, I ran straight up to Sera, her eyes wide. No one stood in my way as I scooped her up and pressed her against me. I buried my nose in her hair, breathing deeply of her scent. My wolf should have calmed down, but he refused to settle. The urge to claim Sera, to cover her with my scent, was almost overwhelming.

"Hey there, wolf," Sera whispered in my ear, one of her hands running through my hair as she ran a soothing touch down my back with the other. "I'm okay. We're all okay."

The wraith screeched in the distance.

All? My eyes shot open, aware again that we weren't alone. "I was worried we'd lost you," I admitted, hearing the emotion grating in my voice.

Em, who stood behind Sera, watched us with somber eyes, standing there quietly. This Em was a far cry from his usual brash self. Just what had happened to him in that punishment tank of Taneisha's?

"We're fine, thanks for asking," Franc replied. "Someone want to explain where the wraith Sera came from?"

Marcos recounted our journey with the false Sera and then the emergence of the wraith remnant from his leg, the sounds of grunting and wailing filling the background of our conversation.

"Talk about a dark passenger," Franc replied, clapping Marcos on the shoulder. "At least it's out now."

"I know. No wonder it hurt so much."

"Hey, big guy," Sera whispered in my ear. "You can let

me go. I'm real and I'm not going anywhere." She didn't push me away. Instead, she kept running her hands down my back, seeming to understand how much I needed her reassurance. "You're pretty shaken up. Is there more to this than a twisted wraith?"

I breathed in her scent deeply once more, and then finally released her. I needed Sera beyond words, but it would have to wait. Not just because she hadn't asked to be claimed, or that we weren't alone. There were still the minotaur and wraith to deal with.

I took a step back, trying to regain my composure. The motion of the creatures continuing their fight caught my eye, but they were still on the far side of the garden and caught up in their own drama to even take much notice of us.

"The fake Sera really upset me. I'm mostly upset with myself for not realizing she wasn't you, although in retrospect my wolf knew something was off. But this could have happened with any of us. And I guess it just messed with my head. I don't know what I'd do if something happened to any of you. You're my oldest, closest friends."

Saying it out loud, I felt like I'd exposed my vulnerable underbelly. Yet every word was true, and I needed them to know. All of them.

"You can't get rid of us that easily," Caden replied, shaking his head. Flower petals and grass showered off of him as he moved. He chuckled, despite the tense circumstances. I couldn't help but laugh along with him. "Besides, we're all back together now."

But for how long? I kept the thought to myself, not wanting to voice it aloud. Ever present in my mind were the mating marks covering Sera's shoulders. What did that mean for Sera and me? For the posse?

I needed a resolution. My wolf was howling in my mind. But how hard could I push this motley crew?

"You're a mess," Franc said, brushing off Caden's shoulders.

"I'm surprised to hear you feel so strongly about the posse," Em said to me, his sedate demeanor belying the intensity I knew lived under the surface. "You've hardly been back since our academy days. Not since you moved back home with your pack. I tried not to take it personally, but I couldn't help feeling like you just had better things to do than keep in touch."

His chastisement rang true, and for a moment, I couldn't find the words to respond.

"Uh, guys?" Sera broke in as the minotaur howled in the background. "I hate to break up this feel fest, but shouldn't we be focusing on the brawling beasts?"

Franc held up his hand. "I disagree. The beasts are preoccupied with their battle and this is more important right now." Sera gaped, but Franc turned to me. "Go on."

I took a deep breath, but then kept on rolling. "You're right, I haven't been back. It's hard to forge a life beyond pack territories. We're expected to stay on clan land. Find a trade to contribute to the pack. Even find our mate within the territory. You can guess my mom harps on the last point the hardest." I laughed, but it sounded harsh and joyless. No one laughed along with me. "I don't think my family forgave me for leaving to attend Goldenbriar, despite the scholarship I'd earned."

"Here, I always envied you for your pack," Marcos said,

his voice kind. "I guess I never considered there were downsides to all of that proximity."

I nodded. "I don't think I've told you of you this before, but there was an accident back home while I was at the Academy."

"What happened?" Sera asked.

"After returning for our second year at Academy, there was a barn fire on my mom's property. She lost her favorite goat, and the structure had to be rebuilt."

"That's tragic, but you weren't even there when it happened," Franc replied.

I ran a hand through my hair. Just how long did I have to explain? Across the glen, the minotaur was huffing and puffing, pounding his fists into the dirt, surrounded by black miasma.

"Out with it," Em said. "Looks like they're winding down."

"Right," I replied. "I may not have been there when it happened, but my older brother, Alfred, blamed the cause of the fire on me. We'd spent time that summer painting that barn, and I'd knocked over a can of turpentine. He claimed I failed to clean it up properly, leaving the barn at risk."

"That's balls," Caden replied. "How could they blame you for something when you weren't even there?"

"They blamed me because Al is a golden boy, and Mom was already upset with me for not being around. It was a bit of a pile on. She's said more than once that if I'd been home, it wouldn't have happened. Even after my years at the Academy, it took years for them to see me as reliable again. Mom eventually forgave me for the barn, but she's never gotten over the loss of her goat, Gertrude."

"Poor goat, but you couldn't have helped the rest, even if you'd been home. Why didn't you come back into the city?" Marcos asked. "We'd have helped you out."

"I know you would have. There were plenty of times I thought about asking for a place to stay, but it's hard when you have a pack. Standard social pressures don't even compare to a shifter's mom's guilt trips." I took a moment to meet their gazes one by one, wanting to make sure they understood the sincerity of my words. "I need you to know I've missed you all terribly, but every time I leave home, Al is full of snide remarks about what's going to break while I'm gone. Or what messes of mine he'll have to clean up after me this time."

An ear-piercing screech rang out behind us, so loud I reflexively covered my ears. The minotaur held the wraith-Sera aloft, his massive arms straining as he roared. The sound of metal shredding filled the air as the wraith ripped in two, black dust pouring out of it, coating the minotaur and a wide swath of area around them. The minotaur choked and spat, shuddered, and then fell to the ground. The wraith turned to dust in his hands.

"Huh," Em said. "That wasn't how I figured that would end."

"Right?" Sera replied with a shrug. "Do you think the minotaur is dead too?"

"Hold on." Franc's focus on the fallen beast. "You guys missed this, but Em can somehow see the maze's illusions. It's how we found the path that led to this garden."

"Neat trick," Caden replied. "What do you see, Em?"

The demi-god of Isis stood there quietly, arms crossed. Em was the picture of calm and poise. Only problem was, that's never how anyone would have described Emrys

Tedros. He was missing the spark unique to his spirit, that spark of irritating but confident, eternal playboy. Even his gold-toned skin had paled. What all had Taneisha put him through, and how long would it take Em to rebound?

When Em spoke, his tone sounded almost bored. "I see a minotaur lying on the ground covered in black dust. I could get closer to see if I'm missing anything?"

"No, not yet," Sera said, smiling encouragingly at Em.

"Do you think we should try to escape? I mean, in case it wakes up, I'd rather be gonzo," Caden said.

"I agree," Franc replied. "If we stick to Sera's plan of following the right-hand path, we should exit on the path you guys arrived from."

"Easy enough, we just need to circle round the minotaur. Let's go." Sera led the way, making a wide arc around the minotaur toward the exit. Sera turned back to me. "Thank you for sharing about your family and the fire."

"Yeah, Liam, that sucks. I wish we'd known," Franc said. He stepped close and pulled me into a rough hug, like he could squeeze his support directly into me. "You'll always have a place to stay with me."

Caden pulled me into a hug next. "I'd offer you a room, but the best I have is my couch. Still, it's yours anytime."

Marcos clapped me on the shoulder. "You already stay with me when you're in town, but I'm glad you shared your situation with us."

Em didn't initiate a hug. Hands on his hips, his face was stern. "You're always welcome in my spare room, too." It wasn't enthusiastic, but that was about the most I could expect out of him in this mood, I suspected.

"Hmm," Sera subvocalized. "Let me see if I have this

correct. Your legacy that we're looking for is a moonstone head which magically connects you to your pack when you're away from them. Is that right?"

"Yes," I replied, my voice low. We'd been so distracted, I hadn't been thinking of my legacy much. I supposed I should, if we wanted to get out of this maze. At least we were most of the way around the knocked out minotaur and almost out of this garden.

"Okay, so it's a connection to your pack, whom you also feel a great distance from emotionally. Unlike the posse, whom you feel emotionally closer to despite the distance?"

I nodded. "That's right. Do you think it's a clue for how to find the moonstone?"

Sera frowned. "I'm not sure. My gut says there's crossed symbology there, but I'm not sure what to make of it. Anyone else?"

Caden cleared his throat. "It's like you're stuck between two lives. The one you made for yourself with us, and the one you were born into. The moonstone wolf is your heart connection, which should be your pack, and maybe it still is? But it also sounds like your heart is here with your posse."

And Sera. My mate changes everything. I didn't say that part out loud. "You're right, but how is that supposed to help me find it?"

Sera shrugged. "Sorry, I'm not sure. Just puzzling it out."

To our left, the minotaur let out a long, low groan. All of us froze.

"Definitely not dead," Em whispered. "I don't think there are any illusions."

"He's a fucking genius," Marcos said to me.

I shook my head. *"Yeah, but he's our genius. We're not all batting a thousand today, but there's nowhere else I'd rather be."*

"Damn straight," Marcos replied.

The minotaur stretched and then turned over onto his side, slowly pushing himself up into a sitting position.

"Should we run?" Caden asked.

"Just keep walking," Franc whispered, which spurred us all into movement.

The minotaur let out a low moan, and Em stopped in his tracks. We all stopped, not sure what was going on.

A bright flash of light appeared between us and the opening in the hedge, which was our exit. When the light faded, Taneisha remained. Her frock of choice in this moment was bubblegum pink, and for all I could tell, was actual bubbles of gum. At least she had the grace to make it opaque.

Somehow, I contained my groan of disappointment. Emrys didn't, but he might not have been trying, either.

"I'm not happy to see any of you right now, either!" Taneisha yelled.

"Since when does she yell?" I asked Marcos. He shook his head ever so slightly at me. We hadn't seen her this upset, or at least this emotional, so far during these challenges.

The minotaur clambered to his feet to our left. He was a good head taller than Franc, who was the tallest of us. The beast let out a low grumble.

Taneisha ignored the minotaur and strode right up to Marcos, pointing a finger in his face. "How dare you bring that denizen of the deep into my maze? What were you thinking?"

Marcos huffed. "That wraith was a hitchhiker. Perhaps you would have noticed if you'd been paying more attention to the crap you've been putting us through?"

Taneisha's cheeks flared scarlet. We'd seen her angry, but never upset like this. *"Tone it down,"* I warned Marcos. *"She's on the edge."*

Marcos shot me a look of warning. *"Good. Then we're not the only ones."*

Great. Just great. This would not end well. If it was such a big deal, why hadn't she shown up when the wraith got loose? Why now?

"I noticed!" she yelled. "I had to come up with a plan to cleanse this space. Since this is your fault, you get to wait it out while I work. However long it takes me is time deducted from your deadline."

"That's not fair," Sera said, stepping up next to Marcos. "Marcos didn't know the wraith was there. None of us did."

The minotaur rumbled as if agreeing with Sera. He stood there, brushing the blackened dust off his arms and chest.

Why wasn't he attacking us? Or Taneisha?

"Doesn't matter. What's done is done." Taneisha raised her hand and snapped her fingers. One eyebrow arched as she grinned at us. A thick fog rolled out from the hedge, faster than before.

Unavoidable.

I rushed toward Sera, terrified of losing track of my mate again. But in two steps I faltered, falling to my knees. The mists rose around us and I fell into blackness.

HOUSE OF MIRRORS

SERA

I woke up mid-stride, running down a tall corridor lined with pale gray marble. The stone was cold under my bare feet, and my off-shoulder neckline and gauzy sleeves did little to ward off the hint of chill in the air.

But what a dress! Layers of silk billowed around me as I came to a stop. The tight alabaster bodice fit snugly, yet it was butter soft against my skin. The ombre skirt transitioned from white into a brilliant midnight blue around my calves, making me look like I'd waded through a lake, but classier.

Too bad I didn't like dresses. Come to think of it, I'd feel more comfortable knee deep in a lake than in this girly frock, but trapped people can't be choosers.

Wait, when did I change clothes? Oh, right. I remembered Taneisha fogging us. She must have knocked everyone out. Was I dreaming now or awake in some new fae universe? Did it matter? Sconces lining the walls radiated a muted candlelight. It was enough to make out the delicately carved molding around the doorways, but not enough to see far into the distance.

The hallway I'd been moving through had a series of doorways, most of them closed. One up ahead of me was open, and I approached it cautiously. Bright sunlight shone in through the open arch, inviting me to investigate further. The smell of jasmine and sea salt clung to the air in a secret garden of manicured rose bushes, grassy knolls, and mossy willow trees. I wandered out into the garden; the grass tickling my feet as the sound of unseen waves hit some nearby shore. Birds flitted back and forth between the trees overhead, chirping with enthusiasm.

What kind of wacky part of the maze was this? Was it just my brain burning through stress cycles, or was there more to it?

I caught a flash of movement out of the corner of my eye a moment before I was swept up into the arms of a familiar embrace.

"Liam!" I cried out.

He held me so tight my feet no longer touched the ground. Liam ran his nose along my shoulder and up my neck, leaving a trail of searing kisses as he went. The combination of the heat of his breath and the tickling texture of his no longer so shortly cropped beard grazing across my skin left me squirming against him.

"You smell like Sera," he growled out, his tongue darted across my skin. "Taste like her too."

Breathless, it took me a moment to find my voice. Unlike my new swanky dress, he was dressed as before in jeans and a soft t-shirt. "I didn't know you would be so happy to see me," I teased. "It's not like it's been that long."

He shuddered against me. "Every time I'm apart from you, I fear it might turn into forever."

I tried to pull away, just a little, but he held me tight. "Hey now, you're okay, I'm okay. We're going to get through this. You'll see. We'll finish these quests, get back everyone's legacy, and then we can get back to our normal lives."

"That's the problem," he growled, pulling back so I could see the intensity of his green eyes. The conviction held within them. "I don't want to get back to a normal life. Didn't you hear me say I don't want to go back to my pack? My life is here now, with you." Liam's gaze raked over me, lingering on my exposed shoulders and neck. "You do not know how powerful my wolf's urge to claim you remains. I'd go to war to win you, Sera." He blew out a long exhalation, his tense body shaking with emotion. "If you were willing, I'd have you as my own. Right here. Right now."

I opened my mouth to say something. Anything. Liam's desire was so strong, all I could do was stare at him, lost in my own feelings. Did I want him? Yes, definitely. But did I want to be mated to Liam? To anyone? How could I know? I rarely knew what I wanted for dinner, much less who I wanted in my life every day.

Liam ran his fingertips across my neck, finding the spot right where my neck met my shoulder. "This is where I'll bite you. It's close to my mating mark, plus it will be easy to reach while I'm buried deep inside of you," he whispered.

Liam kissed the chosen spot. Then he licked my skin, his tongue lightly abrading my flesh. I heard myself panting as I dug my fingers into his sides, pulling him closer. When he bared his teeth and clamped down, I gasped. Liam didn't break the skin or even bite down that hard, yet my body responded, heat pouring off of me like I was caught in a wildfire. I thrashed against him, loving the feel of his erection pressing against my thighs through the thin fabric of my dress.

I wanted more, so much more. I almost egged him on. Why didn't I want him to take me right here, right now? I squirmed again, not so much to get away but to feel the strength of him against me. Liam held me deliciously in place, as if it took no effort. I swore I could feel his beast right under the surface, barely kept in check.

My body and my heart may have wanted Liam to claim me, but my mind knew better. Where was the happily ever after in this story? Our time together was finite, controlled by a possibly insane fae. Could Liam truly live his life away from his pack? Could I somehow defy my family and pick my future?

I couldn't imagine it. Check that. It would be impossible.

I went slack against Liam, defeat eating at my desire. He must have sensed the shift in my emotions, because he pulled away after leaving a few lingering, tender kisses along my shoulder. The spot where he clamped down tingled with a near electric sensation.

"One day you'll ask," he said.

"I wish I had your confidence in life," I replied, hearing the sadness in my voice.

Liam took a step back, his hand holding mine. "Then I'll just have to have enough confidence for the both of us."

A shiver rolled over me as the heat of Liam's touch faded. The silk dress did little to warm me as a strong breeze whipped up around us, blinding me with my hair. I reached up to pull it out of my face, discovering my location had changed.

A flash of panic shot through me. Liam was gone! I stood alone in a library, surrounded by books pulled off of the shelves, scattered about and in stacks on tables and chairs. Had the whirlwind that brought me here done that damage? And where was Liam? I couldn't help but worry about him. I figured he wasn't in danger, at least no more so than the rest of us. But he'd been so distraught. How would he manage losing track of me again?

"You're stunning in that frock." Franc's voice came from deeper within the library.

Surrounded by stacks and rows upon rows of books and shelves, I couldn't make out where he was. "Where are you?" I called.

A white sheet of paper waved in the air like a signal flag. "I'm in the back."

I followed his voice and tiptoed through the stacks. I circled around a pile of magazines, but I knocked over a stack of books which got caught in my skirts.

"Watch your step!"

I thought about picking up the fallen stack, but what was that point? It's not like anything was in its proper place. "A little late for that. Did that whirlwind toss everything around?"

"What whirlwind?" he asked.

I rounded a shelf and came face to face with a disheveled and distracted demi-god. Where he usually looked polished and well put together, now his curly blond hair had fallen forward into his face. His shirt was unbuttoned, the sleeves rolled up, and the fabric rumpled.

He was thumbing through a stack of sheet music he held in his hands.

"I meant the whirlwind that brought me here. Wherever this is? Did it make this mess?"

"I didn't notice one. Also, I made the mess."

"What? Why?"

"I suppose I was bored. I've been stuck in this library for hours? Days? Only the fae knows. It's her illusion? Dream? Dream illusion?"

"No, that makes little sense. It's only been a short while since she sicced the mists on us in the garden."

Franc turned to me, a curious smile on his face. "Then time has run differently for me."

"Huh, okay. But why tear this place up?"

Franc handed me a wine glass. "Take a sip."

"Where did you get wine?"

He scoffed. "I can always find wine, little mage. Even within someone else's imagination. Look at this." He held the sheet music up in front of me.

I sampled the spicy full-bodied red wine as I read a few lines from the top of the page. "That's a burlesque theme song? So?"

"This song is featured in an upcoming show at Velvet. A show that's still in development, I might add." He set down the pages, picked up a book, and handed it to me. "This is the story of how Jasper Jeanneau came into possession of the Eye of the Tiger." He handed me another book. "This book covers the schedule at your shop, Enchanted Grounds."

I set down the glass and flipped through the books. Sure enough, they were as he said. "Okay, that's super weird, and it makes me miss my coffee shop."

"And I, my club Velvet."

"Why do you think these books are here?"

Franc ran a hand through his hair, but the curls refused to settle into place. "I really don't know. I've been looking for clues about the maze or our future trials, but those tales appear to have been conveniently excluded from this exhaustive history of our lives. They may just be here to make us homesick or encourage us to give up."

I set the books back down on the nearest table. "It's like an emotionally entangled maze of stories. Have you seen anyone else?"

His gaze narrowed on me, and he stepped closer. "No one, not until you." He reached up and tucked my hair behind my ear, moving my long raven locks over my shoulder. Franc arched a brow and then ran his fingertips across the place where Liam had had his teeth just moments before. I shivered under his touch. "It looks like you've seen our wolf recently. I take it he's well?"

Heat warmed my cheeks as my mind stepped back through Liam's kiss and almost-claiming bite. "He's fine, although I expect he's upset I've disappeared on him. You know you could be wrong? It could have been Marcos almost biting me."

Franc gave a quick shake of his head. "No, I'm not, and it couldn't. Not that Marcos doesn't want to claim you, it's just he's more patient. Hopefully Liam can spend his time in this place searching for his moonstone legacy, not just pining over mating."

I bit my lip. I suppose that's what Liam and I should have been doing instead of fooling around? From Franc's knowing look, he didn't have any illusions about what we'd been up to. "What's the purpose of this library room, do you think?"

"Transparent distraction tactics?" He clucked his tongue. "Not what I thought was your style, but fine, I'll play along." Franc turned and walked around me, his fingers playing across the neckline of my dress, and then the waistline. "This room's purpose? Hard to say. Could be something random Taneisha threw together. Could be something carefully crafted and integral to our mission. Perhaps both. Whichever, I don't think it's real. No doubt our bodies are back in that garden lying there peacefully." He hummed in approval. "You look breathtaking, although I know this isn't your typical choice."

"You can thank my tailor, our captor."

After he finished circling and admiring my dress, Franc moved in closer. I took a half-step back, knocking over another stack of books. I reflexively jerked back from the falling tower, throwing my unsteady self right into his arms.

Franc had me off balance, in more ways than one. He seemed content to wrap his arms around me and keep me close.

His eyes sparkled, and I swore he was holding back laughter. "You know what I don't understand?"

"Hard to say? It might fill this library."

He chuckled and then cocked his head to the side. "Do you miss Enchanted Grounds?"

"Of course, I do! I love my shop. Love the smell of coffee and muffins. Love the nerdy patrons. I even love the late nights. But you know how that is, right? You love Velvet, don't you?"

Franc raised his brows. "I adore Velvet. You really have

to visit us sometime. During working hours, that is."

"I'm not sure your swanky club is quite my jam, Franc," I frowned. "But I appreciate the invitation."

"When you visit Velvet, I guarantee it will be your jam," he said. "I ask about your shop because I know you can leave here. Taneisha offered to return you home, yet you remain with our posse in her trap. Why?"

I shifted in his embrace, wondering whether to escape his touch or his question. I wasn't sure. Maybe both?

"I don't feel right leaving the posse to the fae's whims. Multiple times now I've been able to help your situation. I don't want things to get worse for you if I leave."

His smile deepened. "Pure altruism? You're a rare gem, mage Seraphina Lowe."

Was he making fun of me? "Uh, thanks? I'm just doing what any other decent person would do."

Franc's fingers ran up my spine, sending chills rolling up my back. "So then, anyone would let me fuck them in the shower, just to be decent and reasonable?"

"Well, certainly not! That was just us letting off some steam and pent-up frustrations after tromping through the Netherworld."

"Steamy on multiple levels." His words were light, but Franc's mood had cooled a few degrees. When he spoke again, his tone was sharp. "And would anyone consider letting not one, but two shifters claim them? Just to be nice?"

I got it. Franc didn't want me hurting his friends or himself. I shook my head. "I don't want to disappoint them or hurt any of you, but I'm really not serious about mating. It's a lot of commitment. Plus, my family wouldn't accept one, much less two mates."

He frowned, his gaze taking on a steely glint. "In moments like these, Seraphina, I'd like nothing more than to turn you over my knee and turn that pretty backside of yours a lovely shade of rose." I gasped, the image all too clear in my mind. I expected to feel indignant, but to my surprise, a flash of heat rolled over me. Then he continued on as if his statement hadn't just thrown me for a tailspin. "So, tell me. What's your opinion of your mating marks?"

It took me a moment to gather my thoughts when all I could think of was his hand on my ass. When Franc arched his brow, I suddenly found the words. "I've said it before and I haven't changed my mind. It's got to be more fae magic. If Taneisha can construct these worlds within worlds, then putting some marks on my back to mess with all of our minds would be child's play."

"Then you've turned both Liam and Marcos down? Unequivocally? So they don't hold out hope?"

"I don't want to..." I started, but I couldn't say the next words out loud.

Lose them. I didn't want to lose them.

The idea of parting ways with the shifters made my stomach ache, and the prospect of never seeing Caden, Emrys, or Franc again sent a wave of nausea rolling over me. "Oh boy," I breathed out.

Instead of holding me tight, Franc let go of me, turning back to his pile of sheet music. "Oh boy, indeed. I suppose I don't have to wonder where that leaves the rest of us?"

"Wait a sec, I..." I searched for the right word, which was suddenly more complicated than it should have been. "I'm fond of each of you. It's just that Liam is pushier and more demanding. You, of all of them, have to see that this connection can't last long term."

Franc was suddenly up in my space again, but this time I didn't back off. "You think, because of my Dionysian heritage, that my life is just carousing and partying? That I lack the ability to stick with relationships long term?"

I paused. Had I made that assumption? Ugh, maybe I had? "No, it's just, why would you want to commit? You throw nightly bacchanals at your club, basically. Why would you want to be tied down?"

Franc sighed and frowned, regarding me with a distinct air of disappointment. "No wonder your magic is so fickle. You're stuck on preconceived limits and full of no's."

"Huh?"

"What you need is a possibility mindset, ma chère. Instead of all the reasons things won't or can't work, consider starting with the goal. The hope. The vision of inspiration."

"You really like to hear yourself talk, don't you? All the dreams in the world won't make something possible."

"I suppose I do, but I also suppose that's what happens when theatrical performance runs literally in your blood."

Franc brought his mouth close to mine until I felt the heat of his breath against my cheek. Instead of kissing me, he brushed a finger across my lips. "One of these days, I'm going to show you the freedom of letting your inhibitions run wild. Uncap that magic flowing through your veins." He spoke slower, hovering just millimeters from me. He trailed his fingers down the bare skin of my arms with the lightest of touches. "Show you what's possible when you're not bottling up every. Little. Spark."

I gasped, hungry for air from the breath I didn't realize I'd been holding.

PEACHES AND CREAM

SERA

One moment I was about to kiss Franc and the next a whirlwind hit me again, tossing me from Franc's arms without a hint of warning.

"No!" I yelled, clenching my hands into fists. That conversation couldn't be over. Franc and I hadn't settled anything. Now I stood in the middle of a gourmet-outfitted kitchen, which was even messier than Franc's library room had been.

"Sounds like a terrible trip?" came Caden's silky voice from behind me. I whirled around, finding Caden dressed only in a black bib apron. Unidentified confections adorned his skin and apron. The words Master Chef were emblazoned across the fabric in bright white, only just legible from the smears of flour, or was it confectioner's sugar, dusting the garment?

"Ready for a taste test?" he purred, waving like a game show host to two bowls in front of him.

I couldn't help but smile just a little. Caden looked so

ridiculous and adorable, it was hard not to. "Why are you naked? Did the whirlwind thing deposit you here without your clothes?"

"I might be a demon, but I'm no primitive and I'm not naked. My clothes are over that chair, where I'm not worried about getting them dirty, so I'm using this handily provided apron. When I found myself here in this fantastically stocked kitchen, I figured I'd whip up a snack in case any of you dropped by. And here you are."

Caden's panty-dropping smile was paired with the perfect dimples which were truly not fair on an incubus. I hadn't noticed them before our trip through the Netherworld, likely because his bad boy persona rarely smiled. At least he was still wearing the necklace that inhibited his demonic influence. He'd have been impossible to resist otherwise.

Who was I kidding? He was temptation enough, even without his powers. Wait, was that chocolate sauce on his chest? Powdered sugar on his nose? Ever since Caden had admitted to living a double life and working undercover, his demeanor had softened. No longer taking on that brash persona around all of us had changed everyone's dynamic with Caden, including mine. I found this current version so endearing and self-confident. It was hard not to warm up to him.

"Lucky me?" I walked up to the counter. I almost leaned against it before I realized the granite slab was covered in something gooey. Were those lumps bits of chopped nuts? I didn't consider myself a neat freak, but this was like a caramel explosion had gone off. "Have you seen anyone else?"

"You're the first, but you've been well worth the wait. That dress is sublime on you darling, and from the creases and rumpling, I'd guess I'm not the first to tell you as much?"

"Thank you," I replied, feeling my cheeks warm in response to Caden's compliments. "I don't love it, but at least it's comfortable. Let's see, I ran into Liam in a garden, Franc in a library, and now you, here. Have you been in this kitchen the entire time?"

"Entire? Well yes, I guess so. I took a brief look around in the hall, but then came back here. Figured we wouldn't be here long anyway, from what Taneisha said? At first I poked around the kitchen for snacks, but then I got bored and, well, I love to experiment, so I figured why not?"

I bet you do.

"This place had a professional ice cream maker, so I figured what was the point in trying to make anything else? I've been through quite a few trials over many hours, but I think I'm really onto something. Here, try bowl number one." Caden spooned up a bite, holding it out to me.

Unwilling to lean over that sticky counter, I walked around to his side, regretting it when my bare feet hit what I assumed was a patch of sugar. Or salt? It clung to the soles of my feet, quickly working up between my toes. Was that a chocolate chip under my heel?

"You really went all out," I said. If I pretended the floor was covered in sand instead of food, it wasn't so bad. "What am I trying?"

He held out the spoon. "This is a sweet cream base with a fudge ripple and toasted pecans."

"That sounds delightful." I leaned in and took a bite from the spoon, the creamy, fudgy flavors blossoming on my tongue. The crunchy texture and nutty pecan flavor were a great pairing. "Hmm, that's fantastic. Definite recommend."

Caden's brows furrowed just a little. "It's good? You're sure?"

"It's amazing, Caden. I mean, it's even better than Harper's Frozen Custard. And I would know, there's a shop entirely too close to my work."

"For a mage, you have some curious occupational hazards," he teased. He grabbed the other bowl, spooning up a bit. "What about this one? It's caramelized peach and bourbon vanilla ice cream."

"Are you trying to kill me?" I asked and then went right in for a taste. The jammy peach flavor exploded in my mouth, followed by the smooth bourbon cream base. "Oh, this one's even better. The bits of fresh peach are tangy and just enough to keep it from being cloyingly sweet."

Caden's eyes sparkled. "You're not just saying that?"

"Nuh uh. Why would I mess with you?" I reached for the bowl on the counter, stealing it before he had time to stop me. "I had no idea you were such an excellent cook."

"I dabble in my free time, which isn't much, but it's something I really enjoy. I think it complements my incubus nature."

I glanced around, and while there were plenty of empty bowls, spatulas, and measuring cups around, the only spoon I saw was in Caden's hand.

"How so?" I asked.

"I wear this necklace so I can operate relatively

normally in society without overwhelming those around me, but my demonic urges to seduce and ravish others never go away. Cooking is just another form of seduction, no? I've found few ever refuse a good meal or decadent dessert."

Was it getting warmer in here? I couldn't help letting my gaze wander all over him, but this time I wasn't focusing on the smears of chocolate. He wasn't as large-framed and muscular as the shifters, nor as tall as Franc, but he was all lean athletic muscle. The apron he wore left little to the imagination, especially the bulge of his swollen erection. My cheeks heated as I met Caden's gaze, realizing he must notice me staring at him. Not that he seemed self-conscious in the least.

"Yeah, that makes sense. Is there a spoon I can use?" I stuttered.

Caden held up the spoon in his hand. "This one?" When I reached for it, he moved it out of my grasp. "Do you want more?"

A tingle spread from my toes upward. I wanted him to hand over the damned spoon, but my stomach was doing flip-flops over his request. By the glint in his very amused gaze, I guessed he wouldn't back down easily. I let out a breathy whisper. "Sure."

Triumphant, Caden moved in with his spoon, scooping up a bite while I held the bowl. He spoon fed me a bite of the peach ice cream, which was just as amazing as the first one, but somehow so much hotter. I couldn't remember a time when anyone had fed me like this. Caden seemed to know the perfect angle of the spoon, the perfect quantity to have in each bite, even the perfect pace. His focused attention and the novelty of the act turned me on more than I'd like to admit. From the twitch of his cock under the apron, I wasn't the only one.

"I don't think this is your first time," I panted, overheating despite the thin layers of my dress.

His grin was back, along with that adorable dimple of his. "You wouldn't believe me if I said it was the first time I'd seduced a mage with ice cream?"

I laughed. "I believe you, but only because you're being so specific."

After he'd fed me two more spoonfuls in a delightfully teasing, slow way, Caden took the bowl from my grasp and set it on the counter beside me. He prepped another spoon and stepped closer, pinning me between the counter and his body, his cock rigid against me. I rocked against him, now craving much more than ice cream.

"I think I need a taste," he rasped.

Caden brought the ice cream covered spoon to my lips, painting them with peach perfection. He swooped in and hesitated before licking my bottom lip, setting my whole body on fire. I leaned into him, urging Caden to give me more. His butterfly kisses left me wanting until I couldn't take it anymore.

Even wearing the necklace, his demonic powers were right there below the surface. Every touch was addicting. I was hooked from the first kiss. Hanging on every second for the next touch. Wanting more. Craving more. Needing more.

"Stop teasing me!" I moaned.

When the spoon painted a swath of peach across my neck and shoulder, I shrieked. "Oh, my gods!"

A flash of red lit up Caden's sky-blue eyes. He spoke with a low-toned growl. "I haven't begun to tease you yet, temptress."

I opened my mouth to argue that he was the tempter, not me, but then Caden's mouth was on my neck, nibbling and lapping up the sweet cream he'd covered me with. When he drizzled my breasts, I sighed as he lightly bit and nuzzled his way across my chest while expertly liberating my breasts from their barely constricting neckline.

"I have an idea," he murmured. Caden scooped up another dollop of ice cream, ate it, and then sucked my nipple into his mouth. The combination of the texture of his tongue, the icy temperature of the ice cream, and the suction of his lips had me mewling for more.

He set down the spoon and chuckled. "What was that? I couldn't quite make out your demands through all that moaning and groaning."

Breathless, I couldn't find the words. Instead, I started hiking up my dress, which, with the length, seemed like it was taking forever.

"Let me assist." Caden managed the task better than I, quickly bringing my skirts up to hip level. A pleased growl followed his sharp intake of breath. "Hmm, I think I just named my new favorite ice cream."

"I thought you had a name for it already?" I asked, reaching around him for the tie on his apron. At least that I found easily enough. Tie undone, the fabric slid off of him and to the floor, revealing his long, eager cock.

"Those were just the ingredients, sweetie." He ran his fingers lightly over my pussy, cupping it possessively. "I'm calling it my Utterly Fuckable Peach," he said, practically growling the words into my ear as he slid his fingers into my folds. I ground against his hand, his touch like a live wire of pleasure against my skin. "I love how wet you are for me."

I sighed in relief, needing more of his touch. I encircled his cock in my hand and gasped. Under his firm flesh, I felt a series of hard bumps not far under the skin. "What are these?"

He grinned. "They're implants." When I cocked my head to the side, he explained further. "Tiny ball bearings."

Distracted by my curiosity, I took a better look. "That's, uh, kinky, and unusual. Did it hurt?"

He shrugged it off. "Sure, but not for long. They're fun. Would you like to weigh in?" he asked, strumming his fingertips along my clit.

"I'll cast my vote for posterity," I said, biting my lip. I'd heard demons' sexual appetites were more extreme than other species, and I wondered what else I didn't know. "Condom?"

He groaned under my touch as I stroked him, absently dragging his cheek up along my neck. "And no, I don't have any condoms. However, my charmed necklace doesn't just dampen my incubus effect. It also acts as birth control."

"Then what are you waiting for?" I whispered, grinding my hips against his hand. "I trust you."

He caught my chin with his free hand and turned me to look into his eyes. "You're sure about that?"

"Yes," I said, and he frowned. "Okay, I definitely trust you not to make up charms on the fly. Now get on with it and fuck me." I emphasized my conviction with a firm squeeze of his shaft. "Give a girl a dream to remember."

Caden didn't take more convincing. He lifted me up and set me on the edge of the counter, devouring me with kisses until I couldn't think straight. He slid his cock against my slick folds, teasing me mercilessly. I dug my fingers into his hips, urging him on. I ached for more, and I tried to shift the angle of my hips to get him inside of me. Caden chuckled at my efforts.

I looked up into blood-red eyes. Perhaps it should have scared me, but the sight only ramped me up further. "Please," I whined. "More?"

"Hmm," he growled. "You know what I'll love more than hearing you beg for my cock?"

"What?" I panted, my hands gripping his shoulders, holding him tight against me.

"Hearing you scream my name as you come."

My breath hitched in my throat as a shudder ran down my body. Caden grinned wickedly, then pulled me off the counter, spun me around, and pushed me forward onto the marble, sending bowls spinning. The surface was cool and sticky against my skin, but it was worth putting up with the mess if it meant he'd stop teasing me. He ran his hands up the backs of my legs, dragging my voluminous skirt up around my waist.

He leaned against my ass, threading his fingers into my hair and then gripping my scalp, turning me to meet his ruby gaze. Caden's cock twitched against my thigh as his other hand found my pussy, slipping a finger deep into me. He opened his mouth to speak, but I cut him off.

He enjoyed begging? "Please, Caden. Fuck me. Hard."

He let out a growl before slamming into me, lighting my nerves on fire. My body strained to adjust to his punishing thrusts, but Caden didn't relent. The steel beads along his cock added to his girth, the sensation more intense than I'd ever experienced.

He drove me out of my mind, gasping for air as I quickly neared my peak.

"Caden!" I gasped, bucking against him, my control on the razor's edge.

The demon slowed his pace and pulled out for a moment, dragging his wet cock across my ass. I sighed when he plunged back into me, my body aching for release. His thumb found my rosebud, now slick from our fluids, and circled it slowly. The unfamiliar, but intense, sensation only inflamed my desire.

Caden's lips nibbled at my ear. "How does it feel to have all of us wanting inside of you? Worshiping you?" he whispered, his hot breath fanning my neck.

"No more teasing!" I demanded.

Caden stopped pumping, his thumb the only part of him moving against me. "How does it feel, Sera?"

I ground against him, rewarded with a twitch of his weighty cock inside of me. Just another thrust, or two, and I could peak.

"Sera," he whispered, bringing my thoughts back to the moment.

As if I could focus on anything but the edge he had me riding on right now? But Caden waited me out, pinning me in place despite my efforts to squirm and grind against him.

"I want it all, okay? I crave all of you." The admission deflated my resistance, crumbling apart my excuses.

Caden rewarded me with another growl and a light bite on my shoulder, rocking into me again. I sighed with relief.

"Good. Because when we're free of the fae's trap, I can't wait to have you in every way imaginable." He slid his thumb into my ass as he quickened the pace of his thrusts. "I want you branded by my touch. Our touch."

His words pushed me over the edge. "Caden!" I screamed out, convulsing against him. A few thrusts later, he let out a grunt and arched against me, his cock pulsing within me. Caden withdrew his thumb and slumped over me, trailing kisses along my shoulders as we floated in a few quiet moments of bliss.

Our breathing ragged, it took me a minute to realize how damp my bodice was. I shifted my weight and Caden lifted off of me, pulling out his still semi-hard erection. Only when I went to stand up did I realize how messy I'd become. I peeled myself away from the marble counter, patches of chocolate and powdered sugar covering my breasts and forearms. My dress had soaked up a puddle of melted ice cream, and my hair was sticky with caramel.

Funny what you didn't notice in the heat of the moment.

Caden twirled me around and pulled me into his embrace. His eyes had returned to their usual light blue and his dimple was back. "I'm afraid I've made a mess of you. And if I have my way, I can promise it won't be the last time."

I smiled back at him as his erection pressed against my thighs through the silk of my skirt. "I could go for round two, but only if I can clean up a little first."

"You're adorable as you are, and you rock this freshly fucked in a bakery look." He planted a kiss on my nose. "Let me get you a damp cloth."

He pulled himself away from me and sauntered over to

the large sinks, not seeming the least self-conscious about his nakedness. I opened my mouth to say something, but a sudden gust of wind knocked me sideways, blinding me temporarily. I clamped my hands over my ears, trying to block out the noise of the whirlwind while hoping for a soft landing.

DOJO

SERA

I got my wish when I landed on a thick padded surface. I was off balance enough to topple to my hands and knees, yet the padding adsorbed my fall.

Marcos' powerful hands scooped me up. He set me back on my feet, but held me tight against him. "Well, well, well. Look who's dropping in for a visit," Marcos said, his deep baritone filling the large, if mostly empty, room.

I couldn't help but smile. "Thanks for the catch."

"Anytime." Marcos returned my smile. "Here, I thought I was alone in this tiny fae universe. I'm happy to be wrong." He took a step back and did a double-take. "This whole look tells quite a story."

I looked down at my chocolate-stained and rumpled dress, feeling my cheeks heat. "I suppose it does. What kind of room is this, anyway?" I adjusted my bodice, feeling the damp fabric stick and peel away from my skin.

He arched a brow, no doubt from my deflection. "It's a martial arts exercise room, which suits me just fine. I checked out some of the adjacent spaces, but they were all more of this, so I ended up coming back here to practice my forms."

I looked around, taking in the room. The large open space was decorated in shades of beige and bamboo surrounded by wooden framed translucent paper shoji walls. A diffused light filtered in through the walls and a stream of incense hung in the air. With every breath, I felt calmer and more centered. It made perfect sense to me that Marcos had ended up in this space, just as the other members of the posse had awoken to spaces that also suited them well.

"At least it's pleasant?"

"I can't complain. The simplicity has given me time to think." Marcos buried his nose in my hair and took a deep breath. "While I've been here alone, I can tell you've been busy. Let's see. I scent Caden, Franc, and Liam on you. In this roughly used blue and white dress, perhaps I should call you Alice?"

I shook my head and laughed. I pulled away from Marcos and sat down on the floor, and he sat across from me. I tried to run my fingers through my hair to get it out of my face, but my hand came away sticky, so I ended up tucking it behind my ears instead. "This sure isn't Wonderland."

"How are the others?" he asked.

Where did I even start? "They're all fine, same as you. I found Liam in a garden."

"Was he focusing on ways to find his legacy so we can get out of this maze?"

"Uh, no. I'm worried he's too intent on claiming me rather than finding his moonstone."

"Understandable," Marcos said. "The urge can be overwhelming, especially when it's denied or delayed."

"You both say you're my mates, so how is it he's so distracted, yet you don't seem to be as overwrought?"

"I'd be a liar if I said mating you, claiming you, wasn't always in my thoughts, Sera. But I know better than to push someone as headstrong as you. Plus, I have faith in fate."

He spoke with such conviction and surety, it took me a moment to gather my response, "You have absolute faith because of the mating marks. I still think they're one of Taneisha's tricks."

"They aren't."

I sighed. This wasn't an argument I could win because we didn't have proven it one way or the other, so I let it drop.

"What was Franc doing when you saw him?" Marcos asked.

"Franc's in a library hunting for clues and drinking wine." I frowned, remembering how our conversation had ended.

"That sounds like Franc. So why the frown?"

"He's upset with me for not making up my mind over... all of you."

"Franc's practically allergic to people denying their passions. So?"

A familiar flush of heat hit my cheeks. "So? He threatened to spank me!"

Marcos chuckled, running a hand over his jaw. "That sounds even more like Franc," he said, his voice a low rumble.

"What?"

"I'm just hoping I have a front-row seat for that show."

My jaw dropped, but I quickly forced it closed. More heat hit my face, as I considered the potential that, if Franc carried through with his threat, that we most likely wouldn't be alone. The mental image had me shifting my position as heat pooled between my legs.

"Neither of those stories explains the state of your dress. It looks like it was once a very fetching dress, by the way."

"Caden and his ice cream adventures happened."

Marcos arched his brow. "I didn't know he cooked. Is he any good?"

"Oh, he's good." I blew out a long breath. "Very good."

Marcos guffawed, almost rolling over. "Did you not learn to eat more than you wore?"

I rolled my eyes at him, but Marcos kept laughing. When he stopped, there were tears in his eyes. "I'll pass on asking for details. You didn't see Emrys?"

"No, not yet at least." Although I didn't say it out loud, not seeing Em worried me. He wasn't in the best mental state post the dunk tank Taneisha had put him through. Of all the guys, he needed the most support, not more time alone with his thoughts.

"How long do you think we've been in here?" Marcos asked.

"I'm not sure. Taneisha said we had to wait things out while she cleaned up after the wraith, so I guess it takes whatever it takes. Why? Do you think it matters?"

"I, for sure, think it matters. The fae gave us three days to hunt down Liam's legacy. Every minute we're in here is another minute ticking down off the clock. I worry she's using this as an excuse to burn down time."

The realization hit me straight in the gut. While I'd been distracted, the clock had kept running. Just how much time had we lost in this odd maze within a maze?

I jumped to my feet and began pacing. "But what can we do?"

"Nothing. It's out of our control. They don't call fae fickle for nothing."

The whirlwind hit without warning, Marcos' concerned gaze haunting me as I wondered where I'd end up next. I could only hope there'd be Emrys. Maybe a shower, too.

A MATTER OF TIME

EMRYS

I awoke with a start. Sera lay curled up against me, her breathing ragged once again.

"Shh, little mage. You're safe." I ran a hand down her arm, then her hip, following the lines of her sleeping form. She sighed, then her breathing quieted. Even unconscious, she'd seemed to take comfort in my touch, which I took as a sign that the fae's spell would eventually lift.

I couldn't tell how much time had passed since the minotaur and wraith had fought, but I'd slept twice, awakening each time with the moon still directly overhead and the skies looking like mid-afternoon. One day? Two? It was impossible for me to know.

When Taneisha had initially fogged us, all the others had passed out. I'd run to Sera, fearing for her if the minotaur returned. Nothing I'd done had awakened the mage, but I'd stayed by her side. I could do that much for her, at least.

Hunger gripped my stomach, but I paid it no heed. I propped myself up on an elbow, again looking around at the four hedge walls surrounding us. Since the fog had dissipated, I'd found us alone, encircled by the walls that now served as our prison. I'd walked them repeatedly, searching for a hidden exit, to no avail.

I did not know why the fae's slumber hadn't worked on me. At first I'd wondered if Taneisha was playing more mind games with me, but as time passed, I became convinced this time things were different. First, the fae didn't periodically stop by to taunt me as she'd done regularly while I was in her timeout zone. And second, my mind wasn't playing tricks on me, looping through scenes over and over.

Here, time played out in a straight line. For the first time in a long time, I was bored, and I loved it. Well, not exactly bored. While my mind calmed, changes in Sera's sleep patterns kept me on my toes. Sleep even felt restorative again. Hunger reminded me that my body was corporeal, and not simply a dream.

All of this felt real. At least, I hoped it was.

I'd gone through Sera's and my backpacks from top to bottom, hoping to find something that might help us out of this situation. My magical resilience did us little good when there was nothing to fight off. Nothing to endure.

Nothing other than time. Plus, I couldn't even ask for a more lovely companion.

Out of nowhere, Sera jolted and then groaned. Her breathing quickened as she stretched her limbs. I moved back, allowing her space to roll over onto her back. When Sera's eyes blinked open, I heaved a sigh of relief.

"At long last, sleeping beauty awakens."

Sera looked at me with confusion, blinked her eyes rapidly, and then appeared even more relieved than I felt. She reached up and wrapped her hands around the back of my neck, forcefully pulling me down into a desperate kiss.

Who was I to complain? Sera conquered my lips with the intensity of an invasion, as if she could reassure herself of my presence through contact alone. When she slowed, it was only to nip at my lower lip.

"I've been so worried about you," she breathed out, placing another kiss on my cheek before she dropped back.

Worried about me? Her words warmed my heart as her kisses had stirred my cock. "And I, you. Your sleep was so dysregulated. You haven't awoken since the fae knocked you out."

Sera reached up and ran her hands through her hair and then felt her clothes. "Was it all a dream?" she whispered to herself, a frown etched across her brow. "How long have you been awake?" she asked me.

"Which time?" I replied, to which she frowned. "When Taneisha fogged you all unconscious, I ran to you. It's been some time since then, but I have no way of knowing how long. I've slept twice myself."

Sera paled and then pushed herself up into a sitting position. I moved closer, wary of her unsteady movements. "That's a lot of time lost to find Liam's legacy. Where are the others?" She looked around us, perhaps expecting them to be nearby.

"I'm not sure. We've been locked in here since you passed out. I'd suspect the others are facing similar circumstances."

"Have you looked for secret passages yet?"

"I have, multiple times, but I found nothing. You're welcome to look, but these walls have held us in here for days. Not that I'd have left you here alone."

Sera bit her lip and then wrapped her arms around me. "You're the one I didn't find in dreamland."

I'd become used to the feel of her sleeping body against mine, but her earlier heated kiss still burned in my mind. "You dreamt of the others?"

She nodded her head against my neck. "All of them but you. I was worried about you because I couldn't find you."

I didn't know whether to be flattered or jealous. Perhaps I'd settle for a little of both. While I'd been watching over her, she'd been dreaming of my brothers, but had been in my arms. Damn, had I moved from first to last place, even in her subconscious?

Sera pulled back and looked at me with serious eyes. "Have you really been okay here all alone? The last time we talked, you didn't seem so sure about what was real or not."

I smiled. "Not entirely alone. You've been here the whole time. And I'm fine."

"Fine, how?"

"Fine, fine. As in, I know this is the real world, or at least a fae realm. Do you know you're out of your dream?"

Sera nodded vigorously, her cheeks turning a fetching shade of pink. "Oh yeah, I mean, I'm not wearing ice cream, so that's a plus."

"Sounds like a pleasant dream."

"It had its moments." She bit her lip. I sort of wanted to hear the details, but knowing I hadn't played a starring role gave me pause.

I pulled away. "I suppose we should try to find a way out of here. Perhaps by working together we'll have better luck."

Sera reached out and pulled me closer to her. "There's no point. The maze will release us only when Taneisha deems it time. Actually, I wanted to thank you."

"Thank me?" I blurted out. "I figured you'd hate me. It's my fault you're on this crazy ride with us."

Emotion welled in Sera's eyes. "There have been moments, sure, but I'm having more fun than I'd like to admit. This is an adventure that'll stick with me for a while when I go back to my normal life."

I ran a hand through my hair, gathering my thoughts. That wasn't the reaction I'd expected from her. "I keep forgetting you've been living outside of supe society. I can't imagine how hard that's been for you."

She shrugged it off, but I could see the pain tensing her expression. "You know, if I'd stayed at Goldenbriar, I'd have asked you out."

"None of the others?" I asked, hating myself after I'd said the words. I might as well have tattooed JEALOUS on my forehead.

Sera bit her lip, her cheeks pinking up again. "Maybe? You were the one who had my attention back then, and you knew it."

I did. We've exchanged so many looks and flirtations, but Sera had never pushed for more. "A mage and a demi-god? Your parents would be scandalized."

"True, but my fickle powers scandalized them, anyway." She leaned closer and ran a hand through my hair before pulling me in close, hovering with her lips almost touching mine. "You were the one I couldn't touch."

I hesitated, wanting to tread carefully. "Could you have dated any of us back then without your parents freaking out?"

"Maybe Liam or Marcos? Shifters are easier to swallow for them. But a demi-god? But you were the one I couldn't have. When you walked into my shop and swept me into the storage closet, I was looking for an excuse to give in and give you whatever you wanted."

My heart skipped a beat. Sera had won over the rest of the posse, but she'd been waiting for me. "What do you want now?" I whispered. I needed her to need me.

"You, golden boy," she said, teasing my lips with her own.

The nickname she'd taunted me with at the academy stirred something primal in me. She was my one who'd gotten away at the peak of our flirtation, and now she'd just opened the door wide. When our lips met, Sera's passion was a potent force calling me into action. I answered her kisses with the same intensity she dished out, sending us rolling onto the soft grass. I landed on top, cradled between her thighs, adoring her touch as Sera worked to free my shirt. I sat up and pulled off my shirt before liberating Sera of hers.

"I almost want to leave on that beautiful black bra," I said between kisses. "I want to taste you."

Sera happily obliged, freeing her full, perfect breasts. I said a silent prayer to the gods, grateful for Sera's gloriously curvy frame to worship.

It was as if she'd released a floodgate, inviting me to

fulfill dreams I'd long since considered beyond my reach. I couldn't get enough of the taste of her lips, the feel of her hands on my chest, the sound of her moaning as I sucked on her nipples. When I moved lower and touched the button of her jeans, Sera eagerly unzipped and shimmied out of them. She grabbed her matching black panties, but I stopped her.

"Allow me?" I asked, lowering myself between her thighs.

"Please," she panted.

I smiled, loving the sight of her undulating under my touch. I laid a trail of kisses across her stomach before nibbling on her thighs, my fingers dancing lightly across the fabric of her panties.

"Tease!" Sera groaned.

I breathed heavily against her panties before I gave in to her demands, pulling the fabric to the side to reveal her swollen pussy. Sera let out a sigh of relief as I ran my tongue down her folds, parting them with my fingers. Her juices coated my lips as I circled her clit with my tongue, penetrating her with two fingers as Sera bucked against me.

I couldn't wait to be inside of her, but watching Sera come apart under my touch fulfilled a silent need I'd carried with me since the moment we'd met.

When her breathing quieted, Sera looked up at me with a wicked smile, beckoning me. I kissed my way slowly up her body, finding her hungry for more. My erection throbbed between us, straining the seams of my jeans. I ground myself against her as we kissed, drawing an animalistic growl from her throat.

"On your back," she commanded.

I was putty in my mage's hands. I rolled over, sliding out of my pants faster than I thought possible as I watched Sera peel off her panties. My cock bobbed in anticipation, drawing her gaze as she straddled me and wrapping her hand around my girth.

"This is more than I expected," she said, leaning in for a kiss as she angled me against her core.

"Happy to surprise you," I replied.

Much as I wanted to thrust up into her, I endured the delicious agony of patiently waiting for Sera to work her way down my length. This kind of torture I'd gladly relive time and time again. None of my dreams lived up to this reality.

Only when I was buried inside her did I allow myself to rock up into her. I let Sera set the slow, steady pace as I gripped her hips. Staring into her eyes as we kissed, I had the sense that she was about to say something, but then lost the words to her building orgasm. I held her tight as she thrashed against me, shooting into her moments later.

Naked, we curled up together on the grassy earth, our breathing slowly returning to normal. I'd resurrected twice in my life, neither of which had been pleasant experiences. Being with Sera, I felt reborn again, knowing implicitly that my life would not be the same after this moment.

"That was a long time coming," Sera said, placing a tender kiss on my arm.

I'd had other lovers, but this was different. My connection to Sera was different. I knew little about fated mates, but I knew with certainty that my future lay with Sera at my side. Now that I'd had her, I'd prove myself to her and keep her. I was hers. I could only hope she was also mine.

"The next one won't be," I replied. It was a promise to us both.

Anyone, or anything, that stood in my way wouldn't be standing for long.

THE SHORTEST DISTANCE BETWEEN TWO POINTS

LIAM

I awoke with the scent of Sera's hair lingering in my thoughts. I shot to my feet, surrounded by a groggy looking Marcos, a slumbering Caden, and a sullen Franc leaning up against the base of a stone fountain.

A quick circle around the group confirmed tall hedge walls locked us in on all sides, and Emrys and Sera were not with us.

"How long have you been awake?" I asked Franc, pacing the grassy length of our confines.

"Long enough to figure out what you've already noticed. Before you ask, no, I haven't seen Sera or Em, and I've only been awake for a short while longer than you."

My beast wanted to pace, growl, and snap. Instead, I strode over to Caden and gave him a firm nudge. "Time to get up." He groaned, then rolled over, swearing in what sounded like demonish.

"What's your plan?" Marcos asked me.

By the look in the panther-shifter's eyes, he knew

exactly how on edge my beast was right now. "My plan?" I asked, trying to focus. I returned to my pacing.

"Yes, your plan," Franc added. "We're in this maze to find your legacy, remember? Therefore, you need to be the one figuring out where and how Taneisha hid it."

"Look, right now I just need to find Sera. Then I can calm down and focus on the rest," I explained.

Marcos pulled himself to his feet and blocked my path. "No, you need to get a handle on your wolf and calm the fuck down now."

"She could be in danger."

Marcos spat on the ground. "No. She's not. Out of all of us, she's handled herself best so far with the fae's challenges. Plus, Taneisha seems to like her. Plus, she's likely with Em. I can nearly guarantee you that our mage is better off than we are right now."

"What if you're wrong?"

Marcos arched his brow, but it was Franc who answered. "He's not wrong, Liam. Can't you see that Taneisha, or her maze, is distracting you from your legacy by keeping you apart from Sera?"

They had a point. Besides, the sooner I found my legacy, the sooner we'd be back with Sera and Em. "Maybe?"

"Don't you think if she's with Em that he'd do whatever he can to protect her?" Franc asked.

"Yeah." I barked out a laugh. "But she's more likely to be the one protecting him."

"Let's all agree not to repeat that to Emrys?" Caden added. Franc and Marcos nodded.

"So? What's your plan?" Marcos asked me.

"I dunno? Get out of this hedge box? Find my legacy and get out of this infernal maze?"

Caden stood up and stretched before he too checked out the wall. "Any ideas on how to get out of this hedge holding cell?"

"Burn it. Machete it. Brute force it."

"Now you're talking," Franc replied, rising to his feet. "After that? Ideas on how to find your legacy?"

I scrubbed a hand across my stubble-covered jaw. "We need to find the center. That's where the prizes in mazes are always found in myths."

"Great idea," Caden replied. "Except how the hell do we find the center when we can't see where we are?"

"Sera had us following the right-hand path," Franc replied. "She talked about it as a game theory method used to solve mazes. If we always stick to the right, then we should find the center, and then the exit."

Caden huffed. "That sounds effective, but hella slow."

The demon was right, and slow was the last thing I needed. I grabbed a backpack and searched through it. "We make our own way through."

Franc loomed over me. "Do you think the fae will allow us to damage her maze?"

"No clue, but we're locked in now. What are our other options?" I pulled out a camp knife. "It's not much, but it's better than sitting and stewing."

Marcos and Caden got to rummaging through their bags as well. After a moment, Marcos held up a lighter. "What about fire?"

"That's a bad idea," I replied. "The flames could take on a life of their own and spread. We could end up burning it down around us."

"Uh, guys?" Caden held up a handful of black vials. "What are these?"

A moment of silence spoke volumes. Franc held out his hand, and Caden handed him one. The demi-god unscrewed the lid and cautiously smelled the contents, disgust creasing his face. "They're definitely not perfume."

"Can we all agree not to drink or touch the gross black substance?" Marcos asked.

"No argument from me," I muttered, holding out my hand for one vial. Caden handed one over and I opened it. "It has to be related to the maze. Otherwise, why would Taneisha have given them to us?"

"Could it just be poison?" Caden replied. "Or a magical curse?"

"Maybe, but that seems obvious, even for the fae," Franc replied. "Plus, she promised Sera not to let us die this time."

In a flash of inspiration, I strode over to the hedge and held up the vial toward the leafy barrier. The wall visibly shuddered, bowing away from the vial. I moved closer, and the hedge retreated where the vial neared. "This is our way through."

Franco moved next to me, holding out his open vial. The hedge reacted the same to his vial, but the effect didn't stick. The hedge moved back into place right after the vial was removed. "We need more surface area," Franc said, smiling with determination.

Caden snapped his fingers. "What we need are flameless torches." He dug into the hedge with his knife, cutting free a couple of branches. Marcos pulled a spare shirt from his backpack and tore it into strips.

As we'd done time after time on school projects

together, we went to work as a team, trimming each branch, wrapping it with fabric, and then drizzling that fabric with the dark contents of the vials. The stench was stomach-turning, but at the end we each had a pair of hedge-repelling tools.

"Not my wands of choice, but if they get us out of here, they'll do," Caden said.

Franc rolled his eyes. "Save us your saucy quips, demon. Everyone ready to try getting out of here?"

We re-packed our backpacks, slung them over our shoulders, and then gathered at the hedge wall.

"Wait, what direction should we take?" Marcos asked.

I pointed overhead. "Toward the moon. It doesn't move. That has to mean something."

"But that makes it not a proper moon. It never sets," Caden replied.

I just looked at him. "Do you always have to be so flippant?"

His brows shot up. "Yeah. Why wouldn't I be? It's my best feature."

"Boys," Franc said, his tone full of warning, holding his branches like a pair of swords. "Onward towards the improper moon?"

We rallied beside him, struggling at first to find a pattern to penetrate the hedge. Franc and I stood back to back, forming our branches into a wedge in front, with Caden and Marcos expanding the wide, v-shape. The hedge, repelled by the potency of the substance on our wands, parted like drapes, allowing us a narrow passage. A few feet into the shrubbery, the path closed up behind us.

"What if this doesn't open up on the other side?"

Caden asked, the edge in his tone echoing the building anxiety within my gut.

"You're not helping," Marcos growled out.

We trudged forward in silence until the greenery parted before us, drawing a collective sigh of relief from all four of us. We were back in the maze proper, lines of hedges leading off into the distance.

Marcos clapped me on the shoulder. "Nice work, wolf. Where to next?"

I walked right up to the next hedge. "I told you. We're going straight through."

"To the moon, boys," Caden chimed in.

This time, no one gave the demon any hell. We moved resolutely together to the next wall, which parted just as slowly yet inevitably as the last one. We passed through two more without problems before emerging into a section where the row was open straight ahead of us.

"Finally," Franc breathed out. "It'll be nice to see further than a foot ahead of us for a bit."

As if invoked purely by Franc's words, we heard a lowing roll through the air, followed by a not unfamiliar stomp to our left.

"Run!" I yelled.

COMING INTO FOCUS

SERA

A sudden crackling noise startled me awake. "What's that?" I whispered.

Em pulled me close against him. "I'm sure it's nothing." For a moment, I hoped he was right, but then the sound came again. Twigs breaking. A shaking of the ground. Voices I didn't recognize. "Hmm, no such luck. Look." Emrys pointed to a spot on the hedge wall surrounding us.

I sat up, pulling myself away from his warmth. "It's open!"

"We should go," Emrys replied, gathering the clothes we'd scattered around us, handing me mine.

We threw on our clothes, our focus on the sound of the ruckus out in the maze. "Do you think it's the others?" I asked.

A roar sounded through the air, stilling my movements.

"If it is, they aren't alone," Em replied, holding my bag out to me. "Hurry."

I grabbed the backpack and threw it over my shoulders, following Emrys to the opening into the maze. I looked in all directions but noticed nothing other than hedges. "See anything special?"

He shook his head. "Which way should we go?" We had three options: left, right, and straight ahead.

"My default has been to stick to the right," I replied. Unfamiliar voices filled the air, coming from the left, changing my mind in a heartbeat. "Left. Toward the voices."

I moved toward the sounds, Emrys staying close by my side. "Do you recognize them?"

"No, but it's people. Perhaps they know the secrets of this place. Or know where things are."

"They might not be interested in helping us," Emrys replied. "Or may be as lost as us."

"Liam's running out of time, Em. Besides, we can't assume everything other than us in this maze is a threat."

"No, just the fae who created it, plus the minotaur. That's all."

"C'mon," I said, eager to follow the voices before they got further away. I jogged along the row, taking a right when I heard the voices carrying. "This way."

Emrys kept up with me as I ran down the row. When the hedge walls opened up into another large open space, I skidded to a halt as the creatures I'd been following finally came into view. The group of four beasts were each over seven feet tall, had broad antlers and long, claw-tipped hands.

"Wendigos!" Emrys hissed.

They were across the way from us on the other side of a large Zen garden dotted with short, carved statues, including satyrs, fauns, and dryads. The white pebbles stood out from the rest of what we'd seen in the maze, and I had to wonder what this place signified.

"This is an oddly chill setting to find a group of monsters," I muttered.

Hearing my voice, the wendigos turning their attention fully toward us, red eyes glowing as they voiced deep-throated growls. They moved around, but didn't come closer to us.

"We should run," Em whispered, his hand on my arm, the slight pressure urging me into movement.

"We followed the voices, but these beasts aren't talking."

"The people must have gone another way," Em said. "Like we need to. Now."

Perhaps I was dumbstruck in fright? So why wasn't I scared? One wendigo separated from the others, walking slowly forward into the garden, his large, bare feet crunching on the white pebbles as he moved. It stopped in the middle and watched us in silence.

"Why aren't they being aggressive?" I asked.

"It's well known that the beasts have an insatiable hunger for human flesh. Perhaps we surprised them? Or perhaps they are waiting for us to run so they can give chase?" Em replied.

I glanced at Em. "So why are they hesitating? And since when do wendigos hunt as a pack? I thought they were solitary creatures?"

He frowned. "What are you saying?"

"They filled this maze with illusions. I think those creatures aren't true wendigos, but just look like them. It would explain why the beasts aren't charging us right now and why there's a group of them."

Emrys seemed to consider this. "You're right, they aren't acting how I would have thought either, but how can we know if your suspicion is right?"

I raised my chin and took a deep breath, meeting his gaze. I pointed my finger at the one in the middle of the garden. "I'm going to meet it halfway and see what happens."

Em's jaw popped as he watched me, no doubt weighing my determination over his desire to pull me away from here. "That's an enormous risk to take on a hunch, especially when your magic is on the fritz. I might defy death, but you don't have that protection."

I just shrugged. "We need to take risks if we're going to win in this maze."

He huffed out a breath. "Fine, but you're not going without me. The guys would kill me if I let something happen to you."

I planted a kiss on his cheek. "I'll be fine. Taneisha likes me, remember?"

He glowered, but slid his hand into mine. "I'm grabbing you and running at the first sign of trouble."

I nodded. We walked side by side toward the wendigo in the center of the maze. The others stepped forward at our approach, but then the near one howled and they backed off. When we got within a few feet of it, the stench of the beast was near overpowering. It stank like the dead, and his labored breath was foul. Yet it just stood there watching us approach.

Not that scary for a depraved eater of human flesh. I

slid off my backpack, not wanting to be encumbered if I was wrong.

"Now what?" Emrys asked. He took my cue and dropped his bag as well.

On instinct, I held up my free hand. "I need to get closer."

The beast raised its hand, mirroring my movements. My curiosity washed away my remaining worries.

"See?" I said to Em. Instead of holding me back, he moved forward with me. When my hand and the wendigo's touched, the sound of tearing paper filled the air and the space between us shimmered, dispelling the image of the wendigo.

Instead of a wild, stinking beast, Liam stood before me, a look of triumph in his eyes. Emrys let go of my hand as Liam scooped me up into his arms, burying his face against my neck. I threw my arms around him, kicking my heels up as he lifted me into the air.

Over his shoulder I saw the wendigo illusions had dropped on the others, leaving a relieved looking Franc, Caden, and Marcos, who were now walking over to join us. They held sticks in their hands and looked sweaty, like they'd been running or something.

"I knew you weren't a naga," Liam growled against me, his whiskers tickling my neck.

"And I knew you weren't a wendigo," I replied.

"I was less convinced," Em added, his smile more at ease than I'd seen since we'd reunited. "But you know it's not like you can stop Sera when she's convinced of something."

Liam pulled back and let me back down, planting a kiss on my forehead as my feet touched the ground.

"Headstrong isn't a strong enough word for our mage. I'm glad you were brave."

"Right back at cha," I said. "I told Em we had to take some risks to win."

Liam smirked. "I'm glad to hear you're open to taking risks," he murmured. "I look forward to witnessing more of your bravery."

I knew Liam meant more than just seeing through the maze's illusions. His focus on mating was absolute, and to my surprise, my resolve was crumbling. Right at this moment, I was so glad to have us all back together. I wanted to keep Liam. All of them. The idea of having to go home without them after the quests were over tore at my heart.

"Nice work, Liam," Franc said. "Sera too. But we're not done yet. We slipped into this garden to avoid that damned minotaur, but considering the lack of exits, now we're trapped in here. We need to keep moving and solve the maze before he finds us again."

"We can't go," Liam replied. He pointed up at the moon, which felt like it was handing directly over our heads. "We've arrived at the center of the maze. This is our destination."

As if on cue, a stomping minotaur trailing smoke out its nostrils appeared at the entrance to the garden.

"Who wants to tell him we've won?" Caden asked.

FALLING INTO CENTER

LIAM

"I will," Sera said, her face a mask of raw determination.

I would have been proud of her if I wasn't so scared on her behalf. "If you think we're going to stand by and let you face down that beast..." I started.

"That's exactly what you're going to do," Sera said, cutting me off. She strode off toward the minotaur, clearly not willing to argue.

I had to run to keep up with her. "Like hell am I going to let you do this alone?"

"Fine by me." She cast a look back over her shoulder. "What are those sticks for?"

I glanced back, seeing we weren't alone. All the guys were right there with us. Emrys was the closest, looking more serious yet relaxed than I'd seen him in a long time. "We used the branches and some magic goo to pass through the hedges."

"Neat trick."

"What's our plan?"

"I'm thinking if you're not a wendigo, and I'm not a naga, then…" she trailed off.

"You don't think it's a minotaur?" Emrys asked.

"That's my point. After all the maze's illusions, we can't know," Sera replied. "We might as well find out if the beast is what it appears. Besides, we're running out of time."

While we'd crossed the garden, the minotaur had entered the space, moving resolutely in our direction. I hoped Sera's instincts were correct. Otherwise, we might be on the verge of fighting the beast.

Sera motioned for us to stop, and we formed an arc facing off against the hulk. Em and I stood to either side of Sera, with Franc to my right and Marcos and Caden to Em's left.

"This seems like an awful plan," Caden muttered.

"Do you have a better one besides running forever?" I replied.

"I'd feel better as a panther," Marcos growled.

"Agreed," I replied. "But let's not escalate things unless he does."

Marcos shook his head, and then we shared a look up and down the line as we watched the minotaur resolutely plod toward us. We were all in need of a shower, a good night's sleep, and a hot meal after the craziness of the maze. I hoped we weren't about to rack up injuries on top of everything else.

The minotaur stopped a few feet in front of us, his sheer mass making me question my plan of action again. But Sera shot me a confident smile, settling my nerves.

I took a half step forward, holding up my hands. "We just want to talk."

Sera moved up with me, giving the minotaur a little wave. "We come in peace!"

"He's not an alien, Sera!" Caden said.

"You're right. I'm not," the minotaur answered, extending his substantial hand. "Name's Ray." His voice was a low, baritone rumble, but he spoke as clearly as any of us.

How had I thought of this person as a monster? Sera elbowed me into motion, breaking me out of my momentary shock. I held out my hand, my breath seizing in my throat as the minotaur closed his hand around mine, and then shook.

He could have easily crushed me, but his grip was gentle. At our contact, a profound change came over the minotaur. Where he'd been wearing only a leather kilt, now he wore tailored khakis and a relaxed t-shirt with the slogan 'keep calm and hoof on' emblazoned across the front. Where his hair had been wild, matted, and hanging into his face, now it was still long, but groomed neatly. Where he'd previously appeared to be snarling, now his expression softened, his eyes kind.

"I'm Liam," I replied, and then introduced the others by name. Ray made a point of shaking everyone's hand.

He was still a hulk of a beast, except now I could sense the empathy rolling off of him.

Sera had been right. Again. I was sure I wasn't the only one in the posse to feel both pride and irritation with her at this moment.

"I'm glad to see you've all finally figured out the maze's tricks and made it all the way to the center garden. I need to show you something. Follow me?" He gestured toward the Zen garden.

"Lead on," I replied.

"It excited me when you first arrived. I get little company here."

"I bet you don't," Sera said. "How long have you been here?"

He grumbled deep in his throat. "Long enough that the illusions have mostly stopped working on me, but I'm not sure exactly. I try to help when I can and when visitors are amenable." He chuckled to himself.

"We appreciate your help," I replied.

He bobbed his massive bull head. "Tell me, what do you seek in the maze?"

"A fae took my legacy and hid it somewhere in this maze." I replied. "It's a precious carved moonstone that connects me to my pack."

"Of course. So it's just your item?" he asked, and I nodded. The minotaur's lips pursed. He stopped, pointing to a spot on the ground next to a rock, which I'd assumed marked the spot. "Stand there."

I moved into position, waiting for something magical to happen, but everyone just stared at me, likely waiting for the same thing.

"All prizes are found in the center of the maze. You are now standing at the center."

For a treasure trove, this Zen garden was pretty bleak. There was the large rock at my feet, the white pebbles in the garden base, a bunch of relatively open space, and my friends surrounding me. "I see nothing."

He laid a heavy hand on my shoulder and then squeezed gently. "Look harder." He turned to the others. "Let's back off a few paces and give him some space."

The others moved away and stood quietly, save Caden

flashing me a thumbs up. I had to admit, this was less scary than facing off against an Azun in the Netherworld, especially now that we knew Ray the Minotaur didn't want to eat us for lunch or crush our bones into dust. The remaining foe we faced was time.

I started my search by looking around and under the rock. Then raking my hands through the pebbles under my feet until I got down to dirt.

When I moved too far afield, the minotaur yelled over. "Stay in the center, lad!"

I sat down on the rock and I looked up at the moon, which was directly overhead. In so many ways, she'd guided my life's journey. My father's token was carved into the shape of a wolf's head from moonstone as a symbol of the moon's influence over our people.

Yet with the full moon ever-present in this maze, why had my beast not felt her usual call? I suppose I'd blamed my wolf's lack of a reaction on this being a fae realm or with time running differently here. But I couldn't remember a time I'd been under a full moon and not had my wolf clawing under my skin to run free in through the night air.

I took another look up at the moon. The moon that never moved. The moon that had served as my guide to the center of this maze. The moon that I realized could be no moon at all.

The moon was the center. Of this maze. Of me.

I shot to my feet, my gaze locked on the moon above. As I stared, a pattern formed over the surface, one I recognized all too well. A wolf's face! The image gained in clarity as I stared, unwilling to look away now that I'd finally located my legacy. Ray had said this is where I'd find it, but was the moonstone unreachable?

I knew it had to be far overhead, yet I reached out my fingertips toward it. I didn't dare look away, lest the image disappear. I willed the moonstone to me, my focus absolute. I would not leave here without it, especially not when I was so close!

My fingers brushed the surface. I strained further and then caught the edge of the carving. Or was it the edge of the moon? My fingers grasped, closing around the cold moonstone, and I pulled it down out of the sky, pulling my hand back to my chest. When I opened my hand, there was my legacy, flashing with moonlight.

I looked up, but there was no longer any moon hanging overhead. It'd been my legacy, hidden in plain sight the entire time.

A murmur roused me from the shock of the feat I'd just accomplished. I turned to my friends, triumphantly holding up the moonstone for all to see.

A scowling Taneisha materialized, her slow clapping punctuating the otherwise silent space.

EPILOGUE - A RECKLESS PATH

SERA

I wasn't sure how Taneisha made her clapping sound so sarcastic. She'd appeared out of thin air with a sour smile plastered on her face. Just how long had she been standing there invisibly watching us? For once she wasn't in some complicated dress, but wore a simple black sleeveless jumpsuit with a vee neck and wide legs. It was such a difference from her norm that I couldn't help but wonder what it meant.

"I suppose I should congratulate you, wolf, except I doubt you would have figured out the solution on your own. Plus, you were so distracted by Sera and your friends, I thought for sure you'd fail." The fae sauntered close to Liam, and suddenly I was in motion, intent on being at Liam's side in case Taneisha pulled something. "Lucky for you, my puzzle had a flaw." Taneisha turned and looked straight at Ray, her eyes sparkling with rage.

"Tany," Ray said. The minotaur's cheek twitched.

"Raymond," Taneisha replied, her voice sharp as steel.

Clearly, they had a history. I had known no one to call

the fae by that nickname, or any nickname except Tink, and he'd never attended Goldenbriar Academy. I might have only been there for two years, but a minotaur would have stuck out like a sore thumb.

"So what's your story?" I asked, coming to stand next to Liam.

"No story. Nothing really," Taneisha said a bit too quickly.

Ray was more forthcoming. "We dated. I was tired of her shenanigans and broke up with her. I asked another girl out for a drink and then next thing I know I'm in here because someone got jealous."

"I was never jealous. It's not my fault you fell into that portal on the way to meet her."

"Uh huh," Ray rumbled.

As they stared each other down, I tried to imagine the two of them together. It left me with so many questions on so many levels, many inappropriate.

"Sounds like you two have a lot to work out," was all I could muster at the moment.

"I want to point out there was nothing in your rules about avoiding interacting with the locals," Liam said to Taneisha. He placed his hand on the small of my back. It was a proprietary and unconscious gesture, and I loved it.

"That's true. I'd forgotten Raymond was in here."

Ray's cheek ticked again, but he just stood there, staring Taneisha down.

I suppose I'd assumed the maze was the minotaur's home, but now I knew better. "Did you trap Ray in here, too?"

Taneisha shrugged with her shoulders and eyebrows. "Maybe."

Ray huffed out a hard-hearted laugh. "Yeah, you did. You also said we'd talk after you cooled off. You're looking ice cold right about now."

I'd expected some sort of witty retort from Taneisha, but she only stared at him. Fae were bound to their word, and I suspected she didn't have an out.

"Oh well. I still almost won," Taneisha said to Liam. "You were down to the wire."

"Only because you put us in that weird dream place!" I exclaimed. "How long were we in that limbo?"

Taneisha tapped her cheek. "Not long enough?"

I clenched my fists, wishing my magic was functional again, even if it was flaky. If it was, I'd have walloped Taneisha right here and now. I was over her playing with all of our lives.

"That I can agree on," Liam muttered, and he shot me a curious look. What had he experienced in that dream-state? He took my hand in his, urging me to calm down, but suddenly all I could think about was the way he'd clamped down on my neck within the dream. "The delay doesn't matter now. We won back my legacy and we're ready to tackle the next challenge together."

"But you can't leave Ray in here. He'll likely spoil the maze for your future victims," I said, giving the fae another reason to let the minotaur out. I figured getting Ray out of here was the least I could do for his aid he'd given us finding Liam's moonstone.

Taneisha sized me up, no doubt wondering at my motives. "You're all strategy, mage. I'm not sure how that move benefits you, but when you're right, you're right." Taneisha snapped her fingers. Not one but two portals opened. I could see her faery glen through one and dark pink neon lights shining through a dark night in the other to a back beat of house music. "That one's for Raymond," she pointed to her glen. "And that one's for the rest of you."

"That's not my home," he grumbled.

"It's but a stepping stone on the path," she replied.

"I'm not going through that portal until you do," Ray said, his voice a low rumble.

Taneisha shrugged him off. "Fine, then you can wait."

"Where does ours lead?" Liam asked.

"Your next puzzle, of course. I admit your little posse has done better than I expected. Three for three so far. But since you managed the first few so easily, for this next round, I'll make it more of a challenge."

While I almost groaned at the prospect, Caden actually groaned. We were down to Franc's and Emrys' legacies. Two left out of the five. Only a few more days with the posse. My posse. And then my life would go back to normal. Which was what I wanted. *Didn't I?*

So why did my heart ache like I was having a panic attack? Liam's hand stroked my back, grounding me and easing my discomfort. I didn't look at him, worried my emotions would surface.

"What are the rules this time around?" Franc asked.

"Simple, the same as always. No cheating. No stealing. One three-day shot."

"What's the challenge?" Marcos asked.

Taneisha's smile was devilish. "This time you're hunting Franc's legacy, a lovely mask of Dionysos himself."

Franc's expression was eager, his eyes gleaming with

anticipation as he glanced through the portal. "It looks like you created a fae version of Velvet?"

She shook her head. "Oh no. That's *your* Velvet, sweetie. Don't you recognize it?"

A panicked look flashed across Franc's face. "Velvet doesn't open unless I'm in attendance, yet the sign is on and I can hear the music blaring from here. Who's in there?"

Taneisha shrugged, her face a mask of innocence. "I'm sure I don't know. I mean, I know some, of course, but I haven't been paying enough attention to keep track of all of them."

Franc's expression transformed with fury. "Why my Velvet, fae?"

Taneisha mocked confusion. "What, I'm not allowed to send you somewhere you love? Really, you lot could learn to be just a skosh more grateful for my small mercies. Besides, what better place to hide such a potent magical item? Of any place in the city, I'm sure Velvet can handle all that raw, godly madness."

"How long has it been open?"

Taneisha held up her fingers, ticking them off and then lowering them again. "At least one day. Maybe two? Possibly three."

When he turned to us, Franc's expression was a storm cloud. "We need to hurry. All that power, all that madness, with no tempering force, is a powder keg waiting for a spark. Taneisha might give us three days, but I'd be surprised if we have one day before my club descends into pandemonium. Assuming it hasn't already."

I knew I wasn't the only one catching Franc's panicky

vibes, but before we could even move, Taneisha continued. "Hold on."

She closed her eyes and rocked her head to the side before snapping her fingers once more. In an instant, all of our clothes changed. Well, all except Ray's. Franc had on a deep burgundy suit, fitting for a demi-god of wine. Emrys looked like the suave, rich boy he was, with an expensive tailored button-down shirt that was just a little too small for his muscular frame, designer jeans, and gold chains encircling his neck. She'd dressed Caden in fancy jeans, but with more of a bad boy edge with a dark red tank top and loose-fitting jacket. Marcos wore a black shirt and jeans with a black leather jacket, no doubt a tribute to his typical bouncer attire. Liam wore a tight dark green tee shirt that hugged his frame and jeans. Everyone's hair looked freshly washed, as if we'd all come straight from the shower, too.

Taneisha had put me in a skintight dress with a strappy, low cut vee bodice and a wrap skirt that barely covered my hips. The pink champagne-colored fabric sparkled with shiny sequins and stones. It was a look guaranteed to turn heads. When the guy's gazes swept over me, I wondered if I might get eaten alive.

"Now that's better. I couldn't send you clubbing without proper attire. I mean, I'm no monster, right?"

I wanted to disagree, but I held my tongue. Knowing Taneisha, if I'd complained, she would have made the dress even smaller. Somehow everyone else kept quiet too, although Ray let out a deep, lowing noise as he stomped his foot.

In that same snap, the backpacks and bags disappeared. I hoped that meant we wouldn't need anything extra, not that Taneisha wasn't just making things harder. But who was I kidding?

"Let's get this show on the road," Franc said, crossing over to our portal. The rest of the guys followed, all except Liam, who remained at my side.

"One more thing," I told Taneisha. "I want my magic back. Right now."

"I thought you didn't even like it?" she replied, her tone bordering on flippant. "Even though it's just a colossal pain in your ass most days? Even though it's just enough to keep you separate from the human world and not enough to fit in with your mage fam?"

Oh, how I wanted to strangle her! "Yeah, some days I hate it, but it's mine. It was never yours to take."

"I didn't," she replied, all wide-eyed innocence. "This maze has a mind of its own. It suppressed you, not me. I'm sure when you leave, everything will be back to normal. Well, with your magic, at least."

"You're not inspiring my confidence, Taneisha," I said.

Her smile was so sugary sweet and vapid, I almost developed diabetes on the spot. "And I should care. Why?"

I needed to teach her a lesson. After the legacies were back, I'd pay her back. Somehow.

Liam tugged on my hand, leading my grumbling, muttering self towards the portal to Velvet and onto our next quest.

THE END

Thank you so much for reading Hidden Hearts! It would

mean a lot to me if you could leave a review. A single line or two makes a big difference for other people when deciding if a book is a good fit for them.

The next book in the series, Reckless Rapture, is available for preorder now.

With three legacies down and two to go, the vengeful fae sends the posse to Franc's club, Velvet, to recover his lost Mask of Dionysos. This time around it's not just a legacy on the line, but also the club itself, including everyone inside. When Sera's wild magic complicates things, will her posse be able to bring her back from the edge?

ALSO BY CANDICE BUNDY

The Stolen Legacy Series

Forbidden Fates

Entangled Essence

Hidden Hearts

Reckless Rapture

The Shadow Series

Shadow in the City, A prequel novella

Twinned Shadow

Poisoned Shadow

Shadow Underground

Caught Between Worlds Series

Smoke and Daemons

(previously published as Daemon Whisperer)

Other Works

Ripples, a novella

Open Rack, a contemporary short

WRITING AS CR BUNDY

The Depths of Memory Series

The Dream Sifter

Dreams Manifest

For a list of my full catalog of available titles, visit my
candicebundy.com/books page.

ALSO BY PIPER FOX

Academy for Reapers: Paranormal Romance

Big Wolf on Campus Series: Wolf Shifter Football Romances

The Stolen Legacy Series: Paranormal Reverse Harem

Midnight Huntress Series: Paranormal Reverse Harem

Alien Warriors of New Dilaria Series: Sci-Fi Reverse Harem

The Ironhaven Pack Series: Wolf Shifter Romances

The Dragon Space Order Bride Series: Sci-Fi Romance

<u>Bears of Crooked Creek</u>: A Bear Shifter Romance Series

<u>Seven Brides For Seven Demons</u>: A Demon Romance Series

<u>Last Warriors of Dilaria</u>: A Sci-Fi Romance Series

The Immortal Blood Series: Vampire Romance

ABOUT CANDICE BUNDY

Candice lives in Denver, Colorado with her son and their cat Newt. A professional hedonist, rabble-rouser, winemaker, and goat-herder, she adores archeology and mythology. Candice focuses on habit hacking to meet minimalist, health, productivity, and positive mojo goals, and sometimes even blogs about it. An unrepentant epicurean, she grows heirloom tomatoes and ferments a variety of sauerkraut, sourdough, kombucha, pickles, and water kefir.

If you would like to know when she has new books out, please sign up for her newsletter here. Email her if the mood strikes you.

For more information:
candicebundy.com
candice@candicebundy.com

ABOUT PIPER FOX

Piper Fox writes steamy paranormal romances for sassy, strong-willed women and the sexy, alpha men who love them.

Follow her on:
Facebook: facebook.com/PiperFoxAuthor
Bookbub: https://www.bookbub.com/profile/piper-fox